The Other Side of it All

ISBN: 978-1-329-73466-1

This is a work of fiction. The names, characters, places, and events are either products of the author's imagination or are used fictitiously, and any resemblance to actual persons, living or deceased, business establishments, events, locales is entirely coincidental.

The Memory Letter

Dear Jordan,

    I'm tired, sort of sick, a little sad, but most of all, I'm completely filled to the brim with satisfaction. And I'm very wired, so this will be very long. Bear with me please, no part of this is unnecessary. I haven't been able to sleep since I got back from Pakistan. Which is normal, I mean, there's a big time change and I only just got back a few days ago. I'm happy to see you again, happy to be home again, happy to see everyone else again too, etc. etc. But I'm a little sad, because I miss the place. Isn't that strange? I think it's strange. Back in February I was all, "Four months?! I don't want to go! Four months...what'll I miss in four months? It'll be such a long time!" Blah blah blah, other concerns, worries, lots of walking around kicking the ground and wondering who would miss me, etc. etc. I wrote so much while I was away. So much. Journal entries, little notes and things for you (which I will give to you soon, once I finish unpacking all of my stuff and manage to find my notebook), and little poems too. The poems are my favorite. Since they're not that great, but they're carefree and I don't want them to be great either because that would ruin the moments that inspired them. At least, to me anyway.

    'Look at you, mountain man.

With your buckets of ice and your worn out sandals.
Carving treats for children, keeping it cool in the heat.
Your rough and worn out hands, working your blades,
carving your ice.
Shaving it down, you make it look nice.
I'll take a red, please.
Thank you, mountain man.'

That one is one of my favorites. I don't really have a point to it, I just loved going out to the streets of one town I was in for a while and seeing this man come down with his wagon filled with ice and these two big blades of his. He whittled that stuff down into little cups and cones with ease. Made it look like a very pretty thing to do. So easy, so fun, so simple. Had me wondering why everyone didn't spend all of their time shaving ice.

Anyway, the reason I'm feeling a little sad right now is because I actually miss Pakistan. So much. I don't even know why, I didn't think it was possible. I mean, I met good people while I was there. Great people, actually. And I did enjoy myself most of the time, despite how I may have initially felt about going. But I never expected to miss it this much. I think talking about it might help, or writing it out I mean. I think I'll tell you what I miss, that might be the best way to go about it. So here I go, and please excuse the length, it's the middle of the night and I'm bound to ramble, so bear with me.

I miss the call for the morning prayer sounding through the streets of every town, city, and village without fail every single morning. I miss the sun coming up over the horizon just as the call started, making sure that as you opened your eyes at the sound, you would be bathed in the most beautiful light. Warmed instantly, wide awake and half asleep all at once.

I miss going out every morning once the prayer ended and walking along the dirt roads and streets, watching as market owners slowly went into their shops, or behind their stands, or pulled their little wooden shacks up in wagons, ready to stand there until sunset that day and make whatever they could. I miss seeing the vegetable men sit down in a chair on the side of the road with a big wooden cart filled with eggplants and onions and chili peppers and ginger roots and much more. Or the fruit men, setting up full displays in the streets, crate after crate filled with plums, apples, apricots, grapes, melons, bananas, and mangos. Everyone loves the mangos. Men and women, some with their heads and faces covered and some without, walking up and down the streets sucking on mangoes that they somehow managed to juice on the inside without peeling by simply squeezing and pressing with their hands. Little kids running around playing with sticky mango juice all over their faces as they screamed and laughed.

I miss the busyness of the streets in some of the bigger cities, the honking, racing around, chaotic driving that somehow manages to be controlled nearly all the time. No accidents. Just speed. Fast fast fast! All of it. Whole families zooming around on little bikes, a baby in her mother's lap while she sits sideways on the bike, right next to her two kids, one of whom is on her husband's lap, in between the handlebars. Nothing odd, nothing dangerous. Everyday life. Just getting around. I miss the giant buses that are full on the inside and on the deck up top so you have people hanging off of the sides as they ride along. All calm and cool. Just another day.

I miss the clothing and jewelry shops that seemed to be everywhere no matter where I turned, mixed in with little slices of home like McDonalds or Subway or Pizza Hut. I miss the local restaurants, some would be cooking their food right outside over a large pit fire. And you'd be able to watch from your little outdoor table with the heat from the fire washing over you and making you feel like you feel like you'd melt into the ground right there. And then the wind from the beach would be carried over for a second or two and you'd feel this great feeling of relaxation. That hot and cool contrast, I miss that too. I miss trudging along during the days, with my clothes sticking to me in the seemingly unbearable heat. I miss looking around and seeing everyone carrying on all the same, especially the kids. The kids running around with dirt and sweat covering their clothes and their faces, but all of them happy. Whether in the city or a little village, the kids were the same. Rich or poor. Finding time to play, to run, jump, scream, fight, kick a ball around, chase stray dogs, be chased by stray dogs, play cricket, climb trees, let off firecrackers in the street. Anything and everything. Every day, no matter where I was, the kids were doing something new. And I miss waiting to see what they'd do next.

I miss sitting on rooftops in the cities with my feet hanging over the edge and drinking cold ice cream sodas from glass bottles and then dropping the bottles down into the little back alleys once I'd finished and seeing them shatter and sprinkle the dirty asphalt with little pieces of dust covered glass.

I miss walking along on the dirt roads in small towns and villages late at night and hearing the wind howl and maybe a stray dog or two barking in the distance. Sometimes an old dog will come out from behind a building and lope alongside you for a bit, and you can reach down and scratch its head and it'll slowly move away and trot off to find some food or maybe another dog to be with. I miss the mountains. The lush green fields bursting bright with flowers for miles and miles, carrying on as far as the eye can see. And if you stand in one spot and stare straight ahead, you can see the flowers slowly melt into the sun in the distance. Some fields would be filled with sugarcane plants and the air smelled so good and sweet, everything in those fields smelled good and sweet actually. You could lie down somewhere in the plants and even the dirt would be warm and sweet and you could close your eyes and drift off for an hour or two and when you woke up you'd wind up smelling like clean earth and sugarcane for the rest of the day.

What I miss the most is the thing I wanted to do the most with you. I miss the little tea shops, which were everywhere. The little stands that would be there all day and all night, on the side of the road, in the middle of a town square, a mile away from a village in the middle of the path so you could stop as you were coming/going from the village. I can't describe to you now or ever how sweet that tea was. You'd never find anything like it here. I missed you the most every night when I got some tea, because I would always imagine you sitting beside me, just as worn out as I was from the day, sipping on hot tea, maybe having a bit of cake, and not saying a word. Just glancing from each other to the completely foreign yet entirely familiar world around us.

I missed you a lot in those moments, and even though I had a couple of pictures of you in my wallet and we talked on the phone once every one or two weeks, it was nowhere near enough. An entire photo album and an endless phone conversation wouldn't have been enough to get me to stop missing you. The more I loved it there, the more I wished that you were there with me to experience it. To indulge in that different kind of freedom, that unpredictability, that simplicity, and that complexity. It was a real thing, a real experience, real feelings, real places, real faces, real people. But even talking about it can't do it justice. The only way that you would completely understand is if you had been there too. You will be, next time. We'll go together, hopefully soon.

We can explore that sprawling world together,

*The buildings in the cities, mosques, malls, apartment
complexes, busy streets, chaos at every turn, that all too
familiar smell of industry all around,*
*The sprawling green fields, the flowers, sugarcane, animals
and insects running and skittering all around, the sweet and
syrupy scents that'll knock us off our feet,*
The burning hot days, and the mild nights,
The cool and relaxed air on the beach.
We'll go end to end without a second thought,
You won't just have to read my writing about it,
You'll be in it, you'll be there soon.
I hope you'll be there soon, hope we'll be there soon.
Hope you're doing well.
I'm sorry for rambling, I'll see you in the morning.

Love,
BooBoo.

The Swinging of the Clubs

The hot Karachi sun burned the back of Atiqa's neck as she crouched down behind a bush, hiding from her older brother, Ashir, who came running around the corner of the house with the water hose in his hand. Atiqa covered her mouth with her hand to stifle her laughter when she saw that Ashir was dripping wet. "Atiqa! I'm gonna get you!" he yelled as he spun around, looking towards Amma's vegetable garden.

Atiqa quietly moved sideways, towards the backdoor of their house, not taking her eyes off of Ashir who now had his back to her hiding spot, he was looking up at their mango tree.

"Probably convinced I'm up there," Atiqa thought to herself with a smile. She stood up slowly, careful not to make a sound, and she started walking quietly towards the back steps. Suddenly, Ashir spun around,

"Got you!" he yelled, before spraying her with the hose. Atiqa shrieked with laughter as the cold water hit her in the face, she tried to cover her face with her hands and wound up getting some water in her nose. She coughed and sputtered, falling to the ground and continuing to laugh and scream as Ashir stood over her, still spraying her with the hose.

"Stop! Stop! I'm sorry!" she yelled as Ashir continued to spray her.

Ashir stopped spraying, "Are you ever going to dump water on me again?" he asked.

Atiqa stood up and pushed her wet hair out of her eyes, "Yes," she said before laughing and pushing Ashir, causing him to slip and fall backwards.

"Atiqa!" he yelled as she laughed and ran through the backdoor and into the house.

Amma was in the kitchen when Atiqa ran in, she turned as Atiqa grabbed her around the waist and hid behind her. She spun around, trying to look at Atiqa before sighing and asking, "Atiqa, why are you all wet?"

"Ashir Bhai sprayed me!"

Amma frowned as Ashir ran into the kitchen, dripping water all over the floor,

"Amma! Look at what she did to me!" he yelled.

"I didn't do anything! He sprayed me first!" Atiqa whined.

"You dumped the bucket of water on me first!" said Ashir as he lunged forward, trying to grab her. Amma swatted Ashir's hand away and reached back, grabbing Atiqa and pulling her around so that she was standing in front of her, next to Ashir.

"I don't want you two playing with water anymore, understood?" said Amma sternly.

"But I wasn-" Ashir began to say before Amma cut him off,

"AND, look at what you both did to the floor," she said.

Ashir and Atiqa both looked down and saw that the kitchen floor was all wet.

"Both of you, go dry off and then come back and mop every drop of water off of my floor. If anybody slips and falls, you'll both catch the end of my stick," said Amma sternly.

Ashir and Atiqa both nodded and went outside to the clothesline to get towels.

"I always get in trouble because of you," said Ashir as he rubbed his face with a blue towel before running it through his hair.

"That's not true," said Atiqa stubbornly as she yanked a large white towel off of the clothesline.

"It is true! What'd you have to run into the kitchen for? Amma hates when we run around inside, you know that," said Ashir.

Atiqa hung her towel back up and looked at Ashir, "You're just mad because she saw you trying to spray me!"

"Am not! You're such a kid sometimes Atiqa."

"I'm the second oldest girl in my class!" Atiqa said angrily.

Ashir hung his towel back up and started walking back towards the house, "The second oldest nine year old in a group of nine year olds, big deal," he said before going inside.

Atiqa ran inside after him, "You're not big either! You're only three years older than I am," she said.

"That's old enough," he said calmly before grabbing a few napkins off of the kitchen counter and getting down on the floor to wipe up the water, "Now shut up and help me clean this up or else I'll tell Amma you didn't do what she told us to do."

Atiqa grabbed a few napkins and got down on the floor as well, wiping in big circles with the wad of napkins, "Where is Amma?" she asked.

Ashir shrugged, "Probably laying down in her room."

After the two of them finished wiping all of the water up off of the floor, Ashir went back outside and Atiqa went to Amma's bedroom. Amma's bedroom was right next to the drawing room, it was the only bedroom that was downstairs, the other three were upstairs. When they'd first moved in, Baba had said that all of the kids would be upstairs and he and Amma would be downstairs, but after he died, it just became a matter of convenience for Amma to have her bedroom downstairs. She had trouble going up and down stairs now, her knees bothered her. Atiqa knocked on the door lightly and she heard Amma say, "Come in."

Atiqa opened the door and went inside.

"Close the door behind you Atiqa, the air conditioner is on," said Amma, she was laying across the bed, with her feet pointed towards the window.

Atiqa closed the door and walked over to the side of the bed, she laid down and curled up into a ball next to Amma who put one hand on Atiqa's head.

"Did you and Ashir clean up all of that water in the kitchen?" she asked.

"Yes, Amma," said Atiqa.

"Good," Amma said before closing her eyes, "I think I'll get up in an hour to make dinner, Zaheer should be on his way here by then."

Atiqa sat up and looked at Amma, "Bhai Jaan's coming?" she asked.

"Yes, didn't I tell you?"

"No! How long is he staying?" asked Atiqa.

"Until the end of the summer, the same as every year. Why do you ask silly questions Atiqa?"

"They're not silly! He just...well, he doesn't seem to like being home. He's always yelling and angry whenever he comes," Atiqa said quietly.

Amma opened her eyes and propped herself up on her elbow, "Your brother loves being at home more than anything Atiqa. And he loves all of you too, did you know that when he sends money every month, he always sends extra in case any of you need something for school or just for pocket money? He just has a bad temper, he's always had it."

"I don't care about money, why does he always get mad at us? He always screams at me and Ashir, sometimes he hits Ashir, and he yells at Tariq Bhai too, he only gets along with Saima Baji," whined Atiqa.

"His money is the only reason we can afford our home and everything else, since your father died, Zaheer's taken care of us, Atiqa. Try to understand, he isn't used to how much younger than him you all are. Even Saima is four years younger than him, and anyway, he hasn't been the same since your father died. I'm sure he feels alone sometimes. The only reason I stopped working is because he threatened to never speak to me again if I didn't, he's always felt like taking care of all of us was his responsibility." Amma sighed and said, "He scares me sometimes."

Atiqa looked shocked, "You get scared of him? But why? You're his Amma..."

"I'm afraid his temper will come back to haunt him one day. That he'll do something reckless. Either with you kids, or with himself..." she trailed off, staring at the wall on the other side of the room.

Atiqa moved towards Amma and leaned down, kissing her forehead, "Bhai Jaan wouldn't do that, Amma. You don't need to be scared."

Amma looked at Atiqa and smiled, "Go on and tell your brothers so that they can get ready, you can play until I get up, then I'll need your help with dinner," she said before closing her eyes.

Atiqa nodded and got off of the bed, tiptoeing out of the room, and closing the door very quietly behind her before running upstairs to her brother, Tariq's, room. She saw him standing in front of the mirror, with no shirt on, flexing his arms. He turned around when Atiqa laughed.

"ATIQA! Can't you knock?!" he yelled.

"You better not let Bhai Jaan catch you doing that!" she said.

Tariq pulled a t-shirt out of his closet, "He's coming?"
Atiqa nodded.

"When?" he asked as he pulled his shirt on.

"Tonight, Amma's going to start working on dinner in an hour. Didn't you know?" she asked.

Tariq shook his head, "Nope. Nobody tells me anything," he grabbed a book off of his bedside table before flopping down on the bed, "You're right though. I'm going to have to work out in secret while he's here," he said with a bit of a laugh.

"Why?" asked Atiqa.

Tariq put his book down and looked at her, "If he catches me, I'll have to deal with this," Tariq clenched his jaw and spoke in a deep voice, "'you think any of that is actually going to do you any damn good? Get over here, lift this table, lift this chair, lift the generator! Can't do it can you? That stuff's no damn good!'"

Atiqa laughed, "Bhai Jaan never exercised?"

"Ha! Ask him that Atiqa, and see if he doesn't completely lose it! He exercised like a maniac, just never did weight lifting or anything like that. Never went to a gym. He always did hundreds of pushups and chin ups and things like that. I remember every morning, before school, he would go out in the garden and swing Baba's clubs for a half hour. He was always doing something physical. He was just never into gyms or anything," Tariq explained.

"Saima Baji told me he would get into a lot of fights," said Atiqa.

Tariq laughed, "Well...I guess. He would start them, he loved showing off like that. He would ask kids if they wanted to see if they could beat him and if they didn't agree right away, he'd bother them until they did. He always won, he never beat anyone up out of anger, but he'd always throw them around and then brag about it. I remember Baji would always tease him because sometimes a bunch of girls would stand around and just watch him. She always said he'd marry the whole neighborhood when he got older. He always hated it when she did that."

"Did he play with you when you were little?"

"Not much no. Amma got busy when I was four or five years old and Bhai Jaan was starting university by then. Baji would come home from school and take care of me, she'd have me sit with her while she did her homework, and then she'd play with me, fix me something to eat, stuff like that. Bhai Jaan would take me places with him though, never if he was with friends, but if he was going someplace by himself, he'd always take me with him. Baji would come sometimes, but he didn't like her coming much. Said he didn't want to parade his sister around in public. I remember one night, I was seven years old at the time, he came home all excited because his friend had let him borrow his bike and he asked me if I wanted to go to the bakery with him. Baji told him not to take me since I was so small, but he said it'd be fine and he took me with him and I sat in between him and the handlebars and we rode all the way to the Blue Ribbon bakery and got this huge chocolate cake. When we got back home,

16

Amma was furious with him, it's the only time I ever saw her hit him. But that was nothing compared to what Baba did when he got home that night, he grabbed that old bamboo stick of his and chased him all around the house with it. Amma stopped tutoring a little while after that, she wanted to be around to watch me herself."

Tariq looked at Atiqa, "You've been with Bhai Jaan on a bike before haven't you?" he asked.

Atiqa nodded, "Once. He took me and Ashir Bhai to Baba's funeral, remember?"

"Yeah, and Baji, Amma, and I all went with Sameer Uncle."

The two of them were quiet for a few seconds before Atiqa asked, "Do you think he misses Baba?"

"Who? Bhai Jaan?"

Atiqa nodded.

"If he does, he doesn't show it," said Tariq.

"I miss him."

Tariq gave Atiqa a small smile, "I do too. I can't believe it's been two years.......do you think Bhai Jaan would take us to visit his grave if we asked him?"

"Hmm...I don't know. We'll have to ask him when he gets here."

Atiqa opened her mouth to say something else but Tariq cut her off, "Listen, I really want to read this before Amma wakes up," he gestured at his book, "She's going to have me and Ashir running all over the place once she does."

"Well what am I supposed to do?" Atiqa whined.

"Go play outside or bother Ashir or something."
Atiqa huffed, got up, and walked out of the room.

"Close the door behind you!" Tariq called after her, but she ignored him and he heard her run downstairs. Tariq cursed under his breath, got out of bed, walked over to the door and closed it. He walked back over to his bed and dropped down to his knees beside it, he opened the bottom drawer of his bedside table and reached inside with both hands, pushing old papers, books, and photo albums around until he found what he was looking for. Tariq pulled out a small photograph, in the bottom right hand corner was the date, printed in small orange numbers, 14-08-2004. There were three people in the photograph, Bhai Jaan, a handsome nineteen year old at the time, stood next to Baba, straight backed, with his hands at his sides, his fingers curled slightly, with a little smirk on his face. He was sporting a thin mustache and was nearly Baba's height. He had on a black button down shirt which was tucked into a pair of dark grey slacks. Baba stood next to him, a couple of inches taller, with a big smile on his face. His beard had been longer and darker back then, he looked big and strong, nothing like the small, shrunken Baba that Tariq remembered seeing in a hospital bed two years ago. Baba had on a sky blue *kurta* with the sleeves rolled up and a sky blue *salwar* to match. In his thick, hairy arms, Baba held a small boy, no older than six or seven years old, who was laughing at the camera. The boy had on a red t shirt with a picture of a yellow duck on it and some clean, white shorts, and in his hand he clutched a small flag of Pakistan. Tariq smiled as he looked at himself in Baba's arms, he turned the photograph over and saw writing on the back. Amma had written in Urdu, using blue ink, "Zaheer, *Miya*, and little Tariq on Independence Day." He stared at Amma's handwriting for a few more seconds before carefully placing the photograph back inside the drawer, on top of an old book Baba had given him on his fifth birthday.

A few hours later, the dining room table was loaded with dishes, one large bowl of *daal*, a platter filled with at least a dozen lamb kabobs, a pot full of white rice, and a small dish of mint chutney. Amma and Atiqa were both running around, getting plates, glasses, and spoons, setting them all on the table neatly. "Where are Tariq and Ashir with the *naan*?" Amma asked.

"I don't know, they left twenty minutes ago, they should be back by now," said Atiqa, as she stuck a serving spoon into the bowl of daal and placed a fork next to the platter of kabobs.

As soon as she said this, they both heard the front gate swing open and a few seconds later, Tariq and Ashir both burst in through the front door, Tariq had a large paper bag in his arms that he placed on the edge of the dining table. He and Ashir were both panting, trying to catch their breath, as if they had just run a marathon.

Amma looked alarmed, "What happened to you two?" she asked.

Tariq waited until he had caught his breath before he answered, "Altaf Hussain got arrested in London, riots are starting all over the city!"

"What?!" shouted Amma and Atiqa in unison.

"All of the stores are closing, we had to stand in line for ten minutes at the baker's oven, people were swarming the place! Everybody wants to get as much stuff as they can so they don't have to leave their houses later on, nobody knows how long the riots will last this time," said Ashir.

"You two ran back?" asked Atiqa.

"Everybody was running," answered Tariq, "they've already closed down everything in the city, the baker closed his place down right after he gave us our *naan*. We had to convince him to stick around for us, he was itching to leave."

"They've closed down everything in the city?" asked Amma, "Atiqa! What time is it?"

Atiqa looked over at the clock in the drawing room, "It's 9:15, Amma."

"Zaheer should've been here by now..." Amma said, "You don't think he got in trouble...do you?" she asked nervously.

All three siblings exchanged dark looks, but none of them said anything. Tariq spoke up after a few seconds, "Amma...he's probably just caught in traffic, you know how it gets when riots start. A twenty-minute drive winds up being a two-hour drive."

Amma nodded, but didn't say anything, the kids watched as she walked into her bedroom. She came back into the dining room with her phone in her hand, her hands trembled lightly as she scrolled down her contacts list until she reached the name, "Zaheer." Nobody said anything as she called the number and held the phone up to her ear, after a few rings, Amma hung up. "No answer," she said quietly.

"He's probably on his bike, Amma. You know how he is, he doesn't answer his phone when he's on his bike," said Tariq reassuringly.

Amma nodded, but didn't say anything, and then she swayed on the spot. Tariq and Ashir immediately moved forward, grabbing her under her arms and holding her up. Atiqa slid the drawing room door open all the way as her brothers helped Amma over to the couch. Amma sat down on the couch, clutching her head and groaning quietly, "He could've called me when he left," she said, "That boy never calls. He doesn't care about how worried I get."

"Amma, he's probably on his way! Bhai Jaan can handle himself, you know that. Don't worry, it's probably just traffic, really!" said Ashir.

"Atiqa, get her a glass of water," said Tariq quietly.

Atiqa ran out of the room while Tariq and Ashir sat down on either side of Amma, "He knows what he's doing, Amma. It's not the first time he's been out while things are bad out there, he's handled worse than this! Remember that one time, right after Baji's wedding, when that party leader got killed and the entire country was going crazy for two weeks?" asked Tariq.

Atiqa came back into the room with a glass of water, she handed it to Amma, who took a small sip and then just held the glass in her hands, "That was different," she mumbled, "your father was still alive back then, he was with him."

"Yes, but Bhai Jaan was the one who picked Baba up from the office, remember? And he got them both home safely. Baba said that people were blocking the exits to the office building, but Bhai Jaan still got him out, remember? There wasn't even a scratch on either of them! Not even a singl-," Tariq fell silent as somebody knocked loudly on the front gate.

Atiqa leapt to her feet to go and see who it was, but Ashir grabbed her and yanked her back down onto the couch. Tariq got up slowly, "Stay here," he said to Amma and Atiqa.

He motioned at Ashir to follow him and Ashir got up, they both walked into the dining room, pushing the front door open slowly.
There was another loud knock and Tariq called out, "Who's there?"

No answer. Just another loud knock.

Tariq stepped out into the yard, moving towards the gate slowly, "Who's there?" he called out again.

A deep voice boomed in response, "Who do you think?"

The feeling of sweet relief swept over Tariq and he couldn't help laughing as he reached out and unlocked the gate. He stepped back as the gate swung open and Bhai Jaan stepped into the front yard. Bhai Jaan was even taller than Baba had been now, just by a couple of inches. His face was clean shaven now, no hint of the mustache that he'd sported ten years ago, and his hair has been cut a bit shorter, but everything else was the same. He looked as handsome as ever, and his face split into a huge grin when he saw Tariq standing next to the gate.

"*Assalamu Alaykum*, Bhai Jaan," said Tariq, as he pushed the gate closed and locked it again.

"*Waalaykumu Asalam*," replied Bhai Jaan, he reached out and placed his right hand on the top of Tariq's head before pulling him into a tight embrace.

Once Zaheer let go of Tariq, the two of them started walking towards the front door, Ashir stood there with a grin on his face, "*Assalamu Alaykum*," he said while Zaheer placed a hand on the top of his head too.

"*Waalakumu Asalam*," said Zaheer, "you've gotten taller!" he exclaimed, he looked at Tariq again, "both of you have."

"Still not as tall as you," said Tariq with a grin.

"You'll get there. Where's Amma?" asked Zaheer.

"In the drawing room, she was really worried about you," said Ashir.

"Damn it, worrying is her automatic response to everything," mumbled Zaheer as he stepped into the dining room, he quickly walked over to the drawing room door and slid it open. "Amma?" he peered inside.

Amma was sitting on the couch with her head in her hands, and she looked up when she heard her name. Relief swept over her face.

"Zaheer!"

"*Assalamu Alaykum*," said Zaheer, he walked over the couch and lowered his head.

"*Waalakumu Asalam*," Amma stood up and placed her right hand on the top of Zaheer's head before pulling him into a hug and kissing his cheek. "What took you so long?!" she demanded as she released him.

Zaheer grinned, "Traffic. They're rioting out there, Altaf Hussain got arrested over in London, did you hear?"
"Your brothers found out when they went out to get the *naan*, I was worried sick! Why don't you answer your phone? What if something had happened? What if somebody had hurt you?"

"Amma, you know I don't talk when I'm on the bike. Would you like to have your oldest son involved in an accident because he was stupid enough to use his phone while on a bike? And you don't have to worry about anyone hurting me, they'd hurt themselves trying," Zaheer said the last part with a bit of a smirk.

Amma frowned and opened her mouth to say something, but Zaheer cut her off, "I'm fine, Amma," he said sternly.

"Alright," Amma said with a sigh.

Zaheer's expression softened a little, "Where's Atiqa?" he asked quietly.

"*Assalamu Alaykum*, Bhai Jaan," said a quiet voice.

Zaheer spun around and looked down, he smiled when he saw Atiqa standing there with a nervous smile on her face, and "Say it louder!" he said.

"*Assalamu Alaykum*, Bhai Jaan!" said Atiqa loudly and Zaheer laughed before placing his hand on the top of her head. "Good!" he squatted down in front of Atiqa and hugged her, giving her a kiss on the cheek.

He straightened up and saw Ashir and Tariq standing near the door, "Either of you eaten yet?" he asked.

They both shook their heads.

"They were waiting for you, we all were," said Amma.

Zaheer looked at Amma, "Well, nobody else is coming are they?"

Amma shook her head.

"Then let's eat," said Zaheer.

Amma chuckled as the four of her kids all moved quickly into the dining room, she followed them, sliding the drawing room door shut behind her.

By 10:30, the dishes had been put in the sink, the leftovers (there hadn't been many) had been put in the fridge, and Zaheer, Amma, Tariq, and Ashir were all sitting at the table with cups of chai in front of them and a package of rusks in the center of the table. Atiqa had fallen asleep on the couch in the drawing room while Amma had been making the chai.

Zaheer grabbed a rusk and dunked it into his tea, he brought it up to his lips and blew on it lightly before taking a large bite, "Finish your chai and take her upstairs," he said to Tariq after swallowing the rusk and taking a sip of chai.

Tariq nodded and drained his cup with three big gulps, he pushed his chair back and went into the drawing room, a few seconds later. He came out with Atiqa draped over his shoulder and carried her upstairs.

Zaheer's eyes followed Tariq up the stairs, "Does he help out a lot?" he asked Amma.

Amma nodded, "As much as he can, he comes home from school, keeps an eye on Ashir and Atiqa if I'm sleeping or busy, does his homework, he doesn't see his friends from school that much. Sometimes he'll go with one of them to the gym, but that's it."

Zaheer finished his tea and beckoned to Ashir, who came over and took Zaheer's empty cup, picked up Tariq's empty cup, and took them both into the kitchen. "He goes to the gym?" asked Zaheer with a bit of a frown, "What for?"

Amma gave Zaheer a small smile, "To work out, I think that's what gyms are for."

"Doesn't need a gym for that," grunted Zaheer.

Amma reached over and put a hand on Zaheer's shoulder, "Not everyone is like you Zaheer."

"Yeah, I know," said Zaheer.

Tariq came back downstairs and sat down in the chair next to

Zaheer, "Bhai Jaan, do you know if Baji is coming to stay for the summer too?"

Zaheer looked at Tariq, "She was planning on coming this weekend, but she'll have to wait till these riots stop now. You can call her tomorrow and ask. Her and that husband of hers'," he said.

"Did you see the picture of Fatima?" asked Amma.

Zaheer smiled, "Yeah, she emailed it to me. Looks just like Saima, except her eyes, she's got his eyes."

Ashir reentered the dining room, "Are you talking about Fatima?" he asked.

Zaheer nodded.

"Are they coming too?" he asked.

"We were just talking about that," said Tariq, "Bhai Jaan said we can call and ask tomorrow morning."

"How come we can't call now?" asked Ashir.

"Power goes out at ten over there, comes back at twelve fifteen, Saima will be asleep by then," explained Zaheer, he looked over at Amma, "That reminds me, did they change the timings here again?"

Amma nodded, "The power goes out for the last time at 5:15 in the evening every day, it comes back at 7:30 and then doesn't go out again until the morning."

"Yeah, but with these riots going on, they'll probably be cutting it a lot more for the next few days. At least until things settle down again," said Tariq quietly.

"Bastards," growled Zaheer.

Amma frowned, "Zaheer!"

"What? When Baba was alive, his friends in the corporation made sure that our district's power never went out that much. He dies and all of a sudden they forget about us. I went and talked to them a couple of times and they said there was nothing they could do, said they couldn't give any special treatment. They're all a bunch of bastards in suits!"

"Zaheer, please, mind your tongue. Your brothers...,"

Zaheer glanced over at Tariq and Ashir who were looking at him, "They know what they can and can't say, Amma."

"Still, I don't like hearing those words coming out of your mouth either."

"Whatever," said Zaheer.

It was quiet for a moment, until Zaheer broke the silence, "You go to the gym?" he asked Tariq.

Tariq quickly glanced over at Amma and then directed his attention back to Zaheer, "Yes Bhai Jaan."

Zaheer smirked, "No wonder you look bigger, but still, you don't need a gym. Remember what I used to do? You could do that."

Tariq nodded, "I remember, Bhai Jaan. But I like the gym, it's just different, gives me a chance to see my friends too."

"Do you work out to be fit or to have fun?" barked Zaheer.

"I-," began Tariq, but Zaheer cut him off, "Look at this, look.

I don't work out like I used to anymore, but look," he got out of his chair and squatted down.

"Zaheer, please-"

"Hold ON, Amma! I'm just showing him, look," he grabbed one leg of the chair and stood up, locking his right arm out in front of him, holding the chair up in the air, perfectly still. His forearm was tensed and he was gripping the leg of the chair so tightly that his knuckles had gone white. Ten seconds passed, twenty, thirty, finally, after thirty-seven seconds, Zaheer put the chair back down on the ground.

"See?! Can you do that?"

"No," said Tariq quietly.

"Then what good is the gym?" asked Zaheer with a bit of a smirk.

"I want to do that too, but the gym is just something different, that's all. Salman Bhai took me for the first time last year and it's just something that I liked, that's all," explained Tariq.

Zaheer flinched when he heard the name, "Salman," and Amma groaned, "Salman took you?" he asked.

Tariq nodded.

"Zaheer, I don't understand what you have against him, he's a perfectly fi-," Amma began before she was interrupted by Zaheer, "What I have *against* him, Amma, is that he is a goof. An idiot. You married Saima to an idiot. That's what I have against him. Saima can do much better than that."

"He takes extremely good care of her, and they have a baby now! It's too late to hate him now," said Amma.

Zaheer laughed, "Takes *care* of her? He was jobless for two years! How is *that* taking care of her? And I have nothing against my niece, just my brother in law. I remember when he came to propose, wearing that tattered old suit of his. Saima deserved better than that, I don't understand what you and Baba saw in him that made you approve."

"Your father thought that he loved her, that he'd take care of her, and he was right, he-,"

"He was JOBLESS, how is that taking care of her?" demanded Zaheer.

"Bhai Jaan, Salman Bhai's got a really good job now. He works for an insurance company now, he makes good money, and he brings Baji here whenever he can. He lets her stay for as long as she wants," said Tariq.

Amma flashed Tariq a look that said, "Don't get involved," but it was too late, Zaheer glared at Tariq, "Are you saying it doesn't make your blood boil? The fact that someone had your big sister live with his parents for two years because he couldn't get a home for them? You don't think she deserves better than that?"

"I do! It's just-,"

"Just WHAT?" boomed Zaheer, "Exactly what is it?" Go ahead, tell me."

Tariq opened his mouth to respond, but before he could answer, the lights went out.

"The power..." said Ashir from somewhere near the kitchen door.

"Bastards," growled Zaheer in the dark.

The old gas lamp that hung near the fridge hissed to life, Amma stood there with a box of matches in her hand.

"Tariq, go turn on the generator," said Amma.

Tariq got up, but Zaheer yanked him back down into his chair.

"Bhai J-"

Zaheer held up a hand to silence him, "Shut up. Do you hear that?" he asked.

Amma, Tariq, and Ashir all stared at Zaheer, "Listen!" he whispered.

Nobody said a word, it was silent for a few seconds, but then the sound of chains rattling and voices cursing came in through the door.

"My bike is outside," said Zaheer quietly.

"Well you chained it up, didn't you?" asked Amma.

"I did, but I left my helmet out there," he stood up, "Looters are getting bold. They're either drunk or they don't know who lives here," Zaheer began walking towards the door.

"Zaheer! Don't!" said Amma.

"I'm just going to go and scare them off," said Zaheer, his jaw was clenched. He looked furious.

Tariq and Ashir both got up, but Zaheer turned around and glared at them, "Stay here. Both of you," he said sternly.

Ashir took a step forward, "But what i-"

Zaheer's hand flew out and whacked Ashir on the side of the head, hard. Ashir stumbled back and his eyes welled up with tears.

"Stay!" barked Zaheer. He opened the door and ran outside into the yard, they heard him open the gate and shout, "What are you DOING?!"

Amma glanced at Ashir and Tariq, Ashir wiped his eyes with the back of his hand and Amma went over to him, she put a hand on his shoulder, "Don't worry. He just didn't want you to get hurt, he'll be back in a minute..." she said.

They heard voice yelling, cursing, and then the sound of something metal crashing against the street.

"I think his bike fell over," said Tariq. He stood up and started moving towards the door, but froze with his hand on the doorknob when another sound cut through the air. A gunshot, a yell from Zaheer, some cursing, and then silence. Tariq threw the door open and ran to the gate, he flung it open and stepped out onto the street. Zaheer's bike HAD been knocked over and a man was laying next to it, his head was bleeding, but he was still moving. Tariq scanned the street and saw a figure on the ground a few feet away, he ran towards it, panic flooding his brain.

"Bhai Jaan!" he yelled as he got close to the figure. He crouched down on the ground next to him and saw Zaheer up close. His face had gone pale, he'd been shot in the stomach, he had his hand over the wound and blood seeped out from in between his fingers.

"Got away," mumbled Zaheer, "The guy got away."

"You're going to be okay, you're going to be alright, just hold on, just..." Tariq's voice trailed off and he stared at Zaheer's face.

There was a scream from behind Tariq and he turned to see Amma running towards them, she dropped to her knees next to Zaheer, pushing Tariq out of the way. She cradled Zaheer's head in her arms.

"ZAHEER!" she screamed.

"I'll be alright, 'M fine. Give me a second..." mumbled Zaheer.

"MY SON! MY SON! SOMEBODY HELP MY SON!"

Tariq heard the sound of running footsteps and turned around, some of the neighbors were running towards them. They stopped next to Amma and Zaheer, "Help me! Help my son!" pleaded Amma.

One of the neighbors, a big, strong looking man, leaned down and gently pulled Amma away from Zaheer, "We'll take him in our car, we'll take him to the emergency room, its' not that far, twenty minutes. You can come with us, come on, quick," he said calmly. Amma stood up and nodded, "Let's go!" she whispered, she leaned down to grab Zaheer, but another man waved her away, "We've got him, Baji," he said.

The bigger man grabbed Zaheer's legs and the other man grabbed Zaheer under his arms. Together, they lifted him up and carried him over to a car parked on the street a few feet away in front of their gate. Amma got in the passenger's side seat and the two men laid Zaheer across the backseat. The big man went around and got in the driver's seat, the other man got in the back with Zaheer, Tariq could see him leaning over, pressing some sort of cloth to Zaheer's stomach. He was about to go over and ask the man if he could go with Amma instead, when he felt a hand on his shoulder. Tariq turned and found himself face to face with an old lady, she had her grey hair up in a bun and a walking stick in one hand.

"Your brother and sister," she said.

"What?" asked Tariq.

"They're alone. My sons will take care of your brother and your mother. Go watch your brother and your sister," she said.

Tariq was rooted to the spot for a few seconds, and then he nodded fast and ran back towards the house. Ashir was at the gate.

"What happened?!" he asked? "Is Bhai Jaan okay? Where are they going? Why was Amma screaming? What happened?!"

"It'll be okay," mumbled Tariq, quickly walking past Ashir, "Close the gate, lock it, it'll be okay. It'll be alright."

Ashir followed Tariq inside, Atiqa had woken up, and she was standing at the foot of the stairs, rubbing her eyes.

"Tariq Bhai? What's going on? People were screaming outside, was somebody fighting?"

"You go back to bed," said Tariq, trying to remain calm, "Go on. It's okay, nothing's happened. Nothing's wrong. Go back to bed."

A buzzer sounded outside and the lights came back on, Tariq rubbed his eyes and looked over at Ashir. Ashir was pale, he looked like he was going to be sick, Tariq fought to keep his voice steady as he spoke, "Ashir, take her to bed. Go ahead, you go to bed too. It'll be okay. It'll be fine, nothing's wrong."

Ashir stared at Tariq for a moment before moving forward and taking Atiqa by the hand, "Let's go," he said quietly.

They started going up the stairs, Ashir looked back at Tariq for a second and Tariq gave him a small smile, hoping it reassured him. Once they were gone, Tariq walked over to a chair and collapsed into it. He propped his elbows up on his knees and stared at his hands. There was a bit of blood on his left hand.

"Bhai Jaan's blood," thought Tariq. Bhai Jaan...he'd gone alone, one of the men had a gun, that's the only reason Bhai Jaan was hurt. But he'd be fine, he'd be alright, nothing could keep Bhai Jaan down. Bhai Jaan was strong, he could handle anything. He'd be alright, he had to be alright...

-Two Years Later-

Atiqa knocked on the bedroom door before pushing it open and going inside, Amma was sitting on the edge of a bed, staring at her hands.

"Amma?"

Amma looked up and smiled when she saw Atiqa, "You're home early today, aren't you?" she asked

"They only had me clean the bathrooms, the bedrooms, and the kitchen today," said Atiqa as she walked over to the bed, "They're having a wedding at the house next weekend, I'll be working all day then. They said they'll pay me twice what they normally pay me."

Amma looked up at Atiqa, "I wish you didn't have to work," she said sadly.

"Plenty of girls my age clean houses for work, Amma. I'm not the only one," Atiqa said matter-of-factly.

"I don't care about other girls, I care about MY girl. You're barely eleven years old..." Amma's voice trailed off, she went back to looking at her hands.

Atiqa frowned when she saw Amma's hands, "Amma?"

"Hmm?"

"Where are your bangles?" Atiqa asked.

Amma didn't answer, instead she kept staring at her hands.

"Amma!"

"I sold them all," said Amma quietly.

Atiqa opened her mouth to say something and then closed it again, she thought about it for a few seconds, and then, "W-why would you do that?" her voice shook a bit as she spoke.

"We needed the money," Amma still didn't look up at Atiqa.

"Amma…Tariq, Ashir, and I, we all work. You don't need to sell your stuff, you don't need t-"

"YES I DO!" yelled Amma, she was looking up at Atiqa now with tears in her eyes, "I have to! I need to! I need to take care of my kids, I need to make sure they're okay, I-I-…" she couldn't finish. She buried her face in her hands and shook with sobs.

Atiqa sat on the bed next to Amma and hugged her, "Amma, don't. You don't need to do anything, yo-"

"I can't. I can't do anything anymore, I can't take care of anyone anymore. I'm broken, Atiqa, I'm broken…" Amma's voice trailed off again and she kept crying. Atiqa clenched her jaw, fighting back her own tears. She saw something move near the doorway out of the corner of her eye, she glanced over and saw Tariq standing there, staring at the two of them. He slowly walked into the room and stopped at the edge of the bed, he crouched down and picked something up off of the floor before standing up again, he stared at Amma, who was now sobbing silently into her pillow.

"I'll make her some chai," he said quietly. Atiqa nodded at him and he turned and walked back out of the room. He closed the door behind him and leaned against it, he held up the thing that he had picked up off of the floor. It was a photograph, a very old one. It was faded and hard to see clearly. It'd been taken in the garden outside, in the photograph was a small boy, no older than eight or nine years old, who was crouching down next to a pair of giant clubs and laughing at the camera. The boy was holding the handle of one of the clubs with both hands, like he was trying to lift it off of the ground. Tariq felt a tear slide down his cheek and he shoved the photograph into his pocket.

The Last Long Walk Down the Lane.

May 29th, 1968

For my last request, I asked that this be given to my family after I am gone, as my final words to them.

It is almost midnight, and I am to be hanged in four hours, before the Fajr prayer. I do not know why. Maybe they believe it will be easier to wash the blood off of their hands if they're able to pray afterwards. I'm not sure and I don't think I would be taken seriously if I asked. I keep thinking about how it all started, how I ended up here. It's been four years since I saw something other than the bars and walls of a cell. I've only been here, in the Condemned Cell, for a little over a month.

They bring you to this part of the prison once your date is close. There aren't many cells here, unlike the main part of the prison, and not every single cell here is full. There are three rows of cells, four cells in each row, each row forming a side to a square. The cells surround the courtyard, which is nothing but dry, cracked ground and pebbles, except for one small tree planted right in the middle, surrounded by a ring of stones. The fourth side of the square is a big, metal wall. There are two doors on opposite walls, the first door is a big door and that's the door that the prisoners, visitors, and guards enter through. The other door is a much smaller door and behind that door is the gallows. Sometimes, if you happen to be awake, you can see them leading a man out of his cell and through that door.

They do their best to carry out hangings either early in the morning or late at night. If other prisoners see them leading someone away, sometimes they'll start yelling, cursing. Not always, but sometimes. Other times there are prayers. Prayers meant to comfort the dead man, prayers meant to insult the guards. As an act of defiance, I suppose. But most times, it's silent. Even if every prisoner is awake and watching, they'll all stay silent, and watch. Then, all you hear is the sound of the man crying as he's being led away, or saying a prayer, and sometimes he'll say nothing at all. When that happens, all you hear is the grunting and muttering of the guards.

Every single man here, all of us, knows that we'll all be led through that door eventually. Five have taken place since I arrived here, I've been awake for all of them. One man struggled, I don't know his name, but he was a young man. Older than me, but still a young man. Maybe in his thirties. He tried to break free of the guards' grip and insisted that he walk himself, so they clubbed him in the back of the head and dragged him through the door instead. There are only seven cells that are full right now, mine included. The cells down here are bigger than the ones in main part of the prison, there's room to walk around, and if I lay down on the floor, my feet don't hit the wall. There isn't anything in the cell except for a bed, just like the cells in the main part of the prison, but we don't need much down here to begin with.

They take you to the toilets five times every day here, before each prayer. And right before your day comes, the guards ask if you would like a shave and a haircut, most men decline. Some, the younger ones, usually accept. Nassir Uncle asked me after supper if I wanted a shave. I declined. He asked if I wanted to cut my hair. I declined. Nassir Uncle is the oldest guard in the Condemned Cell, the unofficial head of this part of the prison. The guards down here respect him and usually do whatever it is that he tells them to do, unless the warden says different. Nassir Uncle is at least sixty four years old, he isn't sure exactly how old he is because he doesn't know what year he was born in, he gave himself a year. All he knows for sure is that his birthday is in September. He has kind, hazel colored eyes and dark, bushy eyebrows with specks of grey in them. His head is shaved and he wears a little black topi. His nose is a little crooked, since he'd broken it once when he was much younger.

He's also the only guard who has shown me any kindness at all since I was brought down here. He gave me books even when I never asked for any and he always tried to slip me some extra food at meal times. The first few times Nassir Uncle tried to bring me books or give me extra food, I reacted harshly. I believed he was showing pity to a dead man and that is one thing that I have never wanted. Not from him, or from anyone else for that matter. I would stay silent whenever he tried speaking to me, and I would knock the extra food out of his hands whenever he tried to hand it to me. Eventually, one day, I asked him what he meant by it all. It was around noon, right before prayer, and he asked me if there was anything I wanted. I stood in my cell, facing him, and asked in a loud voice,

"Haven't you heard, Uncle? I'm a killer! Why are you being kind to a killer? Do you think Allah will reward you for being kind to all of his creatures? Even the ones like me?"

I expected the old man to get angry with me, I expected him to yell for the other guards, maybe even come into my cell and beat me with his stick.

Instead, he gave me a sad smile and said, "Beta, a guilty man does not wait for death as calmly and quietly as you do."

When I didn't say anything, he bowed his head and walked away. I never said I was innocent in front of any of the guards, I never said I was innocent during my trial. I knew there was no point. They wanted to pin the murder on someone, and I was there, even if I denied it, there was no way out for me. But I do not take back what I told my family, I am innocent. I did not kill that officer. I had been the one driving the car, and Vikram was the one who had shot and killed the police officer. Vikram, however, went flying through the windshield when our car crashed. It's hard to charge a man with murder when his brains have been smeared all over the road. Since I was still alive, and I did happen to have a gun on me at the time, I was arrested and charged with the murder. I must make it clear now that I did not know what was supposed to take place. Vikram had told me that we were going to go scare a man who had threatened his sister during the riots, all we were going to do was show the man the gun and tell him to never come near her again. When the officer stepped out of the teashop, Vikram shot him in the chest three times and yelled at me to drive.

I admit that I should've jumped out of the car and made a run for it. I do not know why I didn't and I'm not going to waste time trying to come up with a reason. All I know is that I drove us away from there as fast as I could and when the police gave chase, I kept driving until we crashed. No matter what that police officer did or said to Vikram' sister, I do not agree with what he did. Then again, I never agreed with those riots either. Hindus versus Muslims, Muslims versus Hindus, everyone killing each other over an ancient lock of hair gone missing from a temple. The partition was over twenty years ago now and still everyone is fighting. It's been four years since those riots, but I don't need to step outside of this prison to know that everybody's still fighting over something. A new reason every day. But I'm rambling now, let me go back to where I was; the trial had been quick, as I'd expected it to be. I had a lawyer assigned to me, but even then, I knew I stood no chance.

The officer had been well liked by the people of the city, and his family was present at the trial. His widow, his two baby daughters, his young son, and his parents. I tried very hard to avoid looking over at them, I tried to focus on my family, but whenever I looked over at them, they weren't looking at me. Abba was looking off to the side, his jaw was clenched and there was a vein throbbing in his temple. Mama was staring down at her lap, crying silently. My older brother Yaqeen had his eyes fixed on the back of my lawyer's head. It was only when the trial was over and the guards were leading me out of the courtroom that my family looked at me. All three of them, standing there, watching as they took me away. Abba looking dazed, like he didn't know what he should do. Mama, still crying, with one hand covering her mouth. And Yaqeen, glaring at the guards shoving me along, clenching and unclenching his fists over and over again.

They took me to a jail in the city first, I stayed there for a month before being transferred to this prison. Mama and Yaqeen would visit me every weekend, on Saturday and Sunday afternoons. I told Mama that I was innocent and she said that she knew and then she quickly changed the subject. She never liked talking about where I was or what had happened, it upset her too much. Instead, she would stand outside my cell and spend her visit telling me about what was going on at home. What she cooked on what day, what Abba had done when he had come home from work, how messy the house was, which duas I should recite, and so on. Yaqeen never said much, he would say salam when I was brought to the front cell, he would reach through the bars and place a hand on the top of my head, he would say goodbye and tell me he loved me once the visit was over, and that was about it. Abba only came to see me three times. All three times, he was absolutely silent. He would nod at me when I greeted him and he would wave goodbye as they left. That's it. One weekend, I asked Mama if he was angry with me and Mama said that he wasn't angry, but that it killed him to see me in a cell. She said that he didn't talk much anymore at home, that his demeanor changed whenever my name was mentioned. If she or Yaqeen talked about visiting me in front of him, he would clench his fists and the vein in his temple would start throbbing. I understood, I didn't like it, but I understood. All of that changed once I was transferred.

This prison, the largest in the country, was far away from our city. It took three days to get here by train, and a week if you drove yourself. Mama and Abba weren't able to make a trip this far, so my only visitor was Yaqeen, who came to see me once a month. Now that it was just me and him, he would talk. He would ask me how I was, tell me that everything would be okay, that he had hired a new lawyer to fight my case and that he would have me out soon. He would tell me about his wife and how big she was getting, about what things were like at home, about things at work, how Mama and Abba were. But Yaqeen was always worried, he would always smile and act happy when he saw me, but I could see it in his eyes. Especially on days when I had fresh bruises. The first time he came to visit me, I had two black eyes and a broken nose, he asked if I'd gotten into a fight with another prisoner. He was horrified when I smiled and told him it'd been a guard who beat me.

The guards here beat all the prisoners, not the ones down here very much, but up there in the main prison, everyone gets beaten. Usually, you only have to really worry if you're new. It's their way of breaking you in, of getting you used to the life that every prisoner lives. Other than that, they only do it when someone acts up or if they're in a bad mood and just need a reason to swing their sticks. And most guards are very, very thorough when it comes to beatings. There are a few guards won't do anything more than hit you with their sticks a couple of times to get you to straighten up. But most of them beat you down with their sticks, they punch, kick, and put you in chokeholds. Sometimes, they don't stop until you lose consciousness, or at least stop moving as much. When it's over, they put their caps back on, rub any dirt off of their khaki uniforms, and leave. And you're allowed to crawl back into your cell while one or two watch, or they just throw you back in. If you're beaten very badly, they carry you to the infirmary.

On my first day here, a guard named Amar checked my name and announced loudly that I liked to kill officers. He asked me if I thought I could kill him and I didn't say anything, I just stared straight ahead. So he hit me in the stomach with his stick and when I fell to my knees, he started hitting me repeatedly. Some of the other guards jumped in and they were all swinging their sticks and kicking me, I tried my best to cover up, but it didn't help me much. When it was all over, Amar took me to my cell, spat at my feet, and said, "Welcome to Hell, kutta."

Most of my beatings after that were from Amar, who took a savage pleasure in beating prisoners, especially me. I wasn't beaten as often as some other men were, but whenever I was, he would swing his stick at me as hard as he could. He would yell loudly about how he was doing this for all officers who were in danger of being killed by jackasses like me every day. He said that Allah would reward him greatly for beating a savage dog like me.

Two years ago, the court gave me the death penalty. A letter was sent home to my family, letting them know the date and the time. I wasn't upset when I heard, I knew it would be coming. I knew that they'd give me time, a couple of years to make it seem like I had a chance for an appeal. But I didn't. Nobody ever does. It's all a part of it, nobody dies right away, you hope that something will change in the time that you have. You try to convince yourself that a year, two years, three years is a long time and that something can be done, but deep down you know it isn't true. Deep down, you know that when they tell you the date, no matter how far off it is, you'll blink and it'll be here.

After that, Yaqeen didn't come to visit me again for two months. I thought that he was busy, or that maybe he just didn't want to see me anymore, I didn't blame him. Then, in August of that year, Yaqeen came to see me. After we greeted each other, I asked him why he hadn't been to see me in so long. He didn't say anything.

"Yaqeen, why aren't you answering me?" I asked.

He looked at the ground and mumbled something that I didn't hear.

"What?"

"I..." he looked up at me and I saw that he had tears in his eyes, "I have to tell you something."

"What is it?"

"Abba died."

I remember feeling as though somebody had just dunked my head into a tub full of water. His words were ringing in my ears, but they didn't seem to make sense. They couldn't make sense. I felt like I had forgotten how to stand, so I leaned forward and held onto the bars of my cell with both hands to hold myself up.

"When?" I asked.

"A week after they sentenced you, he was up on the roof and he had a heart attack. We took him to the hospital and he came home a few days later and it was all fine. Then, last month, he had another one while he was praying Fajr. It killed him on the spot."

I stared at Yaqeen and watched as a couple of tears slid slowly down his face. I followed them with my eyes until they reached his jaw, hung there for a second, and then fell to the ground.

"Why was he on the roof?"

Yaqeen gave me a small smile, "After we found out about the sentencing, he went up to the roof and spent the whole day there. Just pacing. He didn't say anything to anyone, he just walked from one end of the roof to the other. He did that everyday up until the first attack."

I swallowed hard and let go of the bars, I stumbled backwards and sat down on my bed. I could feel Yaqeen watching me.

"Mama didn't want me to tell you," he said.

I looked up at him, "What? Why not?"

"She, uh, she didn't think you needed to hear about it when you're already suffering in this place," he said quietly.

We both stared at each other, silently, for about a minute.

Finally, I asked, "How is Mama doing?"

"She's okay. She doesn't talk much lately, but she's fine. Keeping herself busy. To distract herself from it all, I guess. But that's why I haven't visited you, there was the funeral, and I didn't want her to be alone, and-"

I waved my hand to keep him from saying anymore, "Don't worry. I wasn't upset about that, I was just wondering. Besides, those things were more important. I'd be disappointed in you if you came to see me instead. You can't shirk responsibilities, you're the good son," I said with a bit of a smile.

Yaqeen smiled back in a sad sort of way.

I asked him how the funeral had gone and he told me that hundreds of people had come to our house. To pray, to pay their respects, to say good-bye. All of our aunts, uncles, and cousins along with family friends, friends of Abba's, coworkers, and even some old friends from his years in the military. It was dark outside when Yaqeen finally left, before leaving, he promised me that he wouldn't miss any more visits. That night, after roll had been taken and the lights turned off, I laid in my bed and I cried.

I cried all night. I cried because of frustration, sadness, and most of all, guilt. Guilt because I knew what had really killed Abba, what had caused those heart attacks. I remembered Mama's exact words when I had asked why Abba barely visited me at all at the other jail.

"It kills him to see you like this," she had said. It kills him.

The death penalty was what did it. That had been it. He'd kept it all inside of him when I got arrested, during the trial, at the other jail, at home, he'd kept it all inside and he finally broke. He couldn't take anymore, not from me. I had killed my father. It was still dark out when I got filled with the urge to do something. Anything that I could. I got out of bed and stood in the middle of my cell. I thought about how when Yaqeen and I were younger, Abba had tried to get us into fitness and exercising. Every day, he made us do bethaks until our legs gave out from under us. And so, with that in mind, I began doing the exercise.

I did not count the repetitions, I did not plan on stopping. I kept going. Up and down. Bending at the knees, swinging my arms forward, and pushing my hips out as I came back up. Over and over again. I did not stop when the call for prayer sounded, I did not stop when the sun came up, and when Amar called for everyone to line up outside for roll, I kept going.

"Where's the kutta?!" I heard him ask.

I kept going.

I heard footsteps approaching my cell, but I kept going.

Amar banged his stick against the bars of my cell, "Are you deaf now too, kutta? Didn't you hear me call your name?"

I ignored him and kept going.

"Ohhh, you're interested in fitness now? Don't worry, you're a dead man no matter what shape you're in!" he laughed before continuing, "Now, step out of your cell and line up before I give you a beating."

Up. Down. Up. Down. I kept going.

"Have you lost your mind?" Amar growled.

Up. Down. Up. Down. Up. Down.

I heard Amar unlock the cell door and out of the corner of my eye, I saw him burst in and swing his stick at my head. I fell over when it connected and little bright dots erupted in front of my eyes.

"Stupid. That's what you are, you know that? You're a stupid dog. And I'll be glad when you're dead," he spat before walking out of the cell and locking it behind him. "Mark him down! He's in his cell!" he yelled as he walked away.

Once he was gone, I pulled myself up to my feet and touched my head where he had hit me. There was no blood, but there was a big lump there now. I made sure I could stand without falling over before taking a deep breath and resuming my bethaks. I kept going, I don't know for how long, I heard the call for afternoon prayer and I ignored it. I would pay for that later, this was something I had to pay for now. My legs ached and wobbled under me, my lungs burned, I felt sweat pouring down my back and my face, stinging my eyes. But I didn't stop. A little while later, I heard footsteps coming towards my cell again.

"You're at it again?" Amar was back. "I came here to give you your lunch, kutta, but you seem to be too busy to eat."
I ignored him and kept going.

"Ah, we're doing this again. That's fine. I don't have to give you this food, you can starve for all I care."

Up. Down. Up. Down. Up. Down.

I heard Amar drop the tray of food, "You're really starting to make me angry now. You think I've given you beatings before? I'll make sure you never walk again! Stop that. Stop it right now!" he yelled.

Up. Down. Up. Down. Up. Down.

"Okay. You want to test me, that's fine."

He unlocked the cell door again and this time, he hit me in the leg with his stick. I cried out and fell to the ground, instead of leaving when I fell, he pounced. He was on top of me, punching me, hitting me with the stick, pressing my face into the ground. When he finally got off of me, I tried to get back up and he quickly kicked me in the stomach. I crumbled and lay there, gasping for air, I thought I was going to vomit. Amar grabbed me by the hair and pulled me up to my knees, he put his face so close to mine that I could see my own reflection in his eyes.

"Are you done, kutta? Are you done testing me for the day?"

When I didn't say anything, he grabbed me by the throat and choked me.

"ANSWER!" he roared.

I stared at him and when he loosened his grip around my throat, I spit in his face.

Amar let go of me and straightened up, wiping his face with the back of his hand as he got up. I stayed on my knees.

"That," he said as he took his belt off and began wrapping it around his hand, "was a stupid answer."

And then he kicked me in the head and knocked me down again. This time, he was punching and kicking every part of me. My face, my stomach, my head, my chest, my back. Everywhere. Slamming the belt buckle into me. Over and over. It was pointless to cover up. I don't know how long the beating lasted. The last thing I remember is that, when it finally ended, Amar walked out of my cell and yelled,

"Get this dog to the infirmary!"

Seeing his black heels walking away from my cell was the last thing I saw before I lost consciousness.

When I awoke, I was shirtless and laying on my stomach. As the room came into focus, I saw that the place was filled with beds that had crisp, white sheets on them. I also became aware of just how much my body ached all over. I winced as I felt something cold touch my back. I propped myself up on my elbows.

"Oh, you're awake," said a stern voice.

I groaned as something cold touched another part of my back.

"Am I in the infirmary?" I asked.

"That's right."

"And you're the doctor?"

"Well I'm not putting ice on your naked body for fun, am I?"

I felt the doctor peel a cloth away from my lower back and groan.

I turned my head to the side and said, "What's the matter? I'm sure you've seen worse."

The doctor came into view, he was a tall man, bald spot in the middle of his head, and a pair of glasses balanced precariously on the end of his long nose.

"Usually when it's this bad, the man is dead. It's easier to stomach then, all I have to do is clean him up. You, on the other hand, are still alive. Barely. But alive nonetheless."

"When can I go back to my cell?" I asked.

"You aren't going back."

"What do you mean? Bandage me up and send me back. Like you said, I'm not dead."

The doctor walked around to my front and I looked up at him.

"Do you have a death wish?" he asked.

When I didn't say anything, he said, "Don't worry if you do. From what I've heard, you're not here for very long anyway. But, until they wrap that noose around your neck, try to avoid speeding up the process."

"I'd feel much better if I was back in my cell," I mumbled.

The doctor leaned down so that we were face to face, "Amar could've killed you," he said quietly, "If you go back right now, I guarantee you that he will kill you this time. And he won't get in the least bit of trouble for it. You're nothing to anyone here, none of you are. So until I say you can go back, you stay in here. Understand?"

I glared at the doctor for a few seconds before finally nodding slowly.

"Good," he straightened up, "Now that that's settled, I'm going to go get some bandages for you, be right back."

I laid my head on my arms and listened to the sound of the doctor's heels clicking against the floor as he walked away. The pain I was in didn't bother me and I didn't care if Amar's beating left me with a hundred scars either. This was what I deserved. This was my penance.

Yaqeen wasn't the only one who visited me during my time here. Nargis visited me as well. My beautiful Nargis. Every few months, she would tell her parents that she had to go visit a friend, and she would get on a train to come here and see me. If it were up to her, she would come and see me every weekend, but her father would never allow that. It was hard enough for her to visit me as sparingly as she did. She and her family weren't in the country when I was arrested, and by the time they came back home, the trial had already taken place and I was already behind bars. At the jail in our city, she would come and see me every day, despite her father's disapproval. Sometimes, she would be forced to wait an hour or two before the guards finally brought me out and let us see each other, but she didn't care. She would wait, no matter how long it took, she would wait.

Things didn't get any easier when I came here. Sometimes, she would arrive in the morning, and they'd keep her in the visitor area until noon before they finally let her see me. And they would only let us talk for a half hour at the most. Those half hours always seemed like seconds to me. She would always tell me about how things were back home, how her days were going, what things were like at the university where she was a teacher and also a student herself. How much her father kept trying to convince her to break off our engagement and see other suitors.

"What's the use?" he would ask, "That boy was trouble, I knew it. I warned you about him, Nargis! Why can't you at least give Hassan Uncle's son a chance? He's a good boy, he's a few years older than you, he's a surgeon! Can't you see how silly you're being?"

"I don't want Hassan Uncle's son. I don't want a surgeon. I'm already engaged," would be her simple response.

That's what she always said whenever her father brought up the subject of marriage, "I'm already engaged."

Sometimes, I would try to convince her as well, those were never good discussions.

"Nargis?"

"Hmm?"

"Maybe you should think about ending it. Trying someone else."

Whenever I said this, she would give me a wounded look that was quickly replaced by anger.

"I don't want to 'try someone else,'" she would snap.

"I'm no good for you, not like this. Not from in here."

"You're perfectly fine for me, in here or out there. It doesn't matter. I'm engaged to you, I want to be your wife."

"I can't do anything for you from in here, Nargis. Please try to understand."

"I don't need you to do anything for me."

"I can't be with you or protect you or anything, they didn't give me a release date, you know what that mea-"

"I know what it means! Don't worry about that, just don't worry."

And then she would hastily change the subject and talk about our wedding. Where it would be, how many people would attend, what kind of dress she would wear, what henna designs she would get, and so on. I would always listen, nod, and tell her it all sounded wonderful. I never mentioned how unlikely it seemed for any of that to happen, at least, not with me. She could tell, I know she could, because she would always reassure me that everything would be alright.

"You'll get out soon, I know you will. The lawyer Yaqeen hired will get you out, this is just temporary. It's all temporary.

You'll get out and we'll get married and then we'll leave, we'll leave so we never have to remember any of this."

Even after I had been given the death sentence, she insisted that it was all temporary and that I would get out. That there was still plenty of time left. The guards near my cell were always amused by this, I could see it on their faces. To them, Nargis was a stupid girl who was filled with a useless hope. Amar, in particular, took great pleasure in using her to taunt me.

"Looks like our dog has a bitch," he sneered after Nargis visited me for the first time.

Whenever he was in an extremely bad mood, he would threaten to keep her from seeing me again.

"I'll put you in the basement. No visitors allowed down there. How would you like that? Your bitch would be up here, wandering around, looking for you. Maybe I'll have her wait in my quarters, I think she would enjoy that. I know I would."

I never responded, I knew Amar was always trying to get a reaction out of me. Looking for any reason to beat me, and part of me was afraid as well. I wasn't sure if he was serious about throwing me down in the basement or not, but I didn't want to risk not being able to see Nargis or Yaqeen anymore. He would keep taunting and taunting and when he got no response, he would spit onto the floor of my cell before leaving.

During her final visit two weeks ago, I finally convinced her to break off our engagement. She didn't put up a fight, she was crying silently, not saying anything.

"Your dad will be happy," I said quietly.

She looked up at me and I grinned, "I won't be happy," she whispered.

"Nargis..."

"I won't be. I can wait, I will wait."

"Wait for what? There's nothing left to wait for, you know that."

"We'll do something, Yaqeen will do something! You'll get out and then we'll leave, we'll go somewhere far away. We won't be near this place ever again, it will all seem like a bad dream!"

I laughed and she glared at me, "What's so funny?"

I shook my head and smiled at her, "You're talking about waiting for me to get out and we're both standing in the condemned cell, meeting for the last time."

A few more tears slid down her face and she smiled, "You're an ass."

"I know. Make sure whatever guy you wind up with is the complete opposite of me, you'll be less stressed that way."

She let out something that sounded like a laugh and a hiccup before leaning forward and putting her face close to the bars, "Are you scared?" she whispered.

"No."

She sighed and looked down, "I hate this. I hate that we were here and that all of this happened. I wish we could've been somewhere else, I wish we could've been other people."

"All of this isn't because of who or where we are, or even what happened. It's just bad luck, bad luck and my own decisions."

"But you didn't k-"

"I know I didn't kill him. But I didn't say no when Vikram asked me to drive, I didn't even run when I saw him shoot. I could've, but I didn't."

When she didn't say anything, I leaned against the bars and said, "I thought about you a lot, have I ever told you that?"

"What?" she looked up at me.

"I knew. I knew that I wouldn't be able to be with you again, but thinking about it helped. Imagining it helped. Remembering the way things used to be, that helped a lot. Especially on the bad days."

When she still didn't say anything, I continued, "I used to think of that old picture a lot, do you remember? The day I proposed? When I asked you to meet me in that little alley so that we could talk and after I proposed, I took that picture of you. Do you remember it?"

She gave me a small smile and then nodded, "Yes, I do. I still have it."

I grinned, "You had put your hair up and you were trying not to smile, covering your mouth with your hand. Leaning back against the wall, pulling your legs up onto the crate you were sitting on...it doesn't feel real anymore. Feels like a dream," I said quietly.

Nargis stared at me for a few seconds and then she put her hand against the bars, "I wish they'd let you out of your cell. Just for a little while.

I placed my hand against hers' and smiled. In between the cold, steel bars, I felt the warmth of her hand against mine. It was the first time in so long that I'd felt a touch so soft and warm. No threat behind it. No stick or belt swinging my way. If I had closed my eyes in that moment, it would've felt like everything was back to normal. I wouldn't be in this cell, Abba would still be alive, I would be at home, and I'd be getting ready to be married. But that's not how things were. Nargis was here with me, but she might as well have been a million miles away. And at the end of her visit, as I watched her walk out through the big door, it finally sunk in that I would never see her again.

Yaqeen had received the same message as Nargis, notifying him to come and meet me for the last time before the hanging. He came to see me three days after Nargis. I cannot remember the last time I saw my big brother looking so drained. His face looked like it was sagging and his hair was a mess, it looked as if though he'd been running his hands through it for hours. And his shoulders were hunched, as he if were about to fall forward any second.

"Assalam-o-Alaikum," I said when I saw him.

He gave me a weak smile and nodded his head.

"Are you sick?" I asked.

"No."

"Well you look terrible."

"I, uh, I haven't been sleeping much lately."

"Why not?"

"I've been thinking too much," he was rocking back and forth on his feet as he said this.

"Yaqeen."

He looked at me and I saw that he had tears in his eyes.

"I don't know what I'm supposed to say to you," he said quietly, "What kind of stupid thing is this? 'We're going to hang your brother in three weeks, come see him for the last time!'" he kicked at a mound of dirt on the ground.

"You're worried about me?"

"What kind of a question is that?!" he asked angrily.

"Yaqeen..."

"Don't. Don't do that, don't start with me. Don't tell me not to worry, don't tell me it'll be okay, that it'll all be fine. That you're going to a better place. Don't give me that! It shouldn't be you, you didn't do anything!"

Tears were sliding down his face now and we were both staring at each other.

"I should've done something," he whispered, "I should've been there."

"What could you have done? Knocked the officer out of the way when Vikram shot at him? Or maybe you could've stopped the riots before they even started? It's not your fault, it's nobody's fault."

"But I let you-"

"'Let me?' What'd you 'let' me do? You didn't let me do anything. You didn't know what would happen, nobody did. You had your wife. You had your job. You did what you could do, Yaqeen. You've always done whatever you could do for me."

He wiped his eyes with the back of his hand and shook his head, "You know, I always thought you'd live to be a really old man. One of those old men that seem like they've been around forever, for everything. I always thought that I'd be the one to go first."

"You got to arrive first, it's only fair that I get to leave first," I said with a grin.

A smile tugged at the corner of Yaqeen's mouth, "Ass," he muttered and we both laughed.

Once we stopped laughing, he began rocking back and forth on his feet again.

"I didn't want to come," he said suddenly, "I didn't want to come see you for the last time, but now I don't want to leave. I want to stay here until it happens."

I nodded, "I'd like that. But bhabi would run up here and get rid of me before the guards could if I kept you away from her for too long."

Yaqeen chuckled and went quiet again.

I watched him kick the dirt at his feet for a few moments before I finally said, "Take care of yourself, Yaqeen."

He looked at me and nodded, "You too."

"And take care of Mama, and bhabi, and your daughter, and Nargis too, if you can."

He nodded again, he was struggling to find something to say, I could see his jaw was clenched and, just like Abba, there was a vein throbbing in his temple. Yaqeen kept his eyes on the ground as he started to walk back towards the entrance, he turned around to look at me once last time. He was crying, I could tell.

Before he got to the door, I called out, "We'll see each other soon, yeah?!"

Yaqeen ran his hand through his hair before nodding his head and waving at me. The last thing I saw before the door shut was him crouching down against the wall.

After Yaqeen left, I started pacing in my cell. I went from the door of my cell to the wall, and back again. Seeing Yaqeen cry had upset me very much, I held myself together in front of him in order to avoid upsetting him even more, but it hurt to see my big brother cry because of me. I hadn't seen him cry since we were kids, and even then it wasn't this kind of crying. He had looked so hopeless, so tired, and so overwhelmed. I sat down on my bed and held my head in my hands.

I was still thinking about Yaqeen when I felt someone watching me. I looked up and felt myself go numb. Mama was standing there, a white scarf covering her shoulders and the back of her head, she was watching me through the bars of my cell with a small smile on her face. I quickly got up and rushed over, I clutched the bars and stared at her. Her hair had turned grey since the last time I had seen her, and she seemed smaller, like she had shrunk. So much older, so much more fragile now.

"You came?" I asked.

"I couldn't miss the chance to see my son for the last time," said Mama.

"You look older, Mama."

Mama smiled, "So do you," she said before reaching through the bars with a trembling hand and putting it on the side of my face. "You've grown your beard out," she whispered as she slid her hand down the side of my face, stroking lightly under my eye and down over my beard to my chin.

I nodded and she smiled again before moving her hand back up, stroking the small scar above my left eye with her thumb.

"This is new," she said as she touched the scar, "Do you have a lot of these?"

"They didn't hurt, the guards here don't know how to hit. I'll bet I could beat them all in a fight," I said with a grin.

Mama slapped the side of my face lightly and chuckled, "Always playing the hero, you never learn," she said.

She started to pull her hand away and I grabbed it with both of my hands while leaning forward and pressing my forehead against the bars.

"Mama, I...I'm sorry," I tried to blink back my tears but it didn't work, I felt them sliding down my face anyway.

"Kiyoon? You didn't do anything."

"I've caused you so much pain, and Abba too. If it hadn't been for me, he'd be here. And those poems I wrote and sent home to you, the things I carved, I shouldn't have done that. It was hard enough, everything was bad enough, and I made everything worse. I made it all worse!"

Mama reached into the cell with her other hand and placed it on the back of my neck while leaning forward and pressing her forehead against mine. She made shushing noises while squeezing my hands and rubbing the back of my neck.

"Koi baat nahi, koi baat nahi," she whispered, "I'm proud of you and your Abba was proud of you too. You've been so brave, you've always been brave. Rahim just had a weak heart, it was his time, but he loved you until the end. And your writing didn't hurt us either, those poems are going to be like treasure for me. Those poems are going to help me remember you once this is all over, I'm going to hear your voice in those poems, your thoughts. You have nothing to apologize for, absolutely nothing."

I kept crying and Mama took her hand off of my neck and used it to wipe away some of the tears, "Enough of this," she said, "this won't help. It's okay, Syed, everything's okay."

Finally, I let go of her hand and wiped my eyes with the back of my hand.

"I keep thinking about what you always used to say," I said.

"And what's that?"

"That everyone dies."

Mama smiled and reached up to wipe her own eyes, "I've been thinking about that too. It isn't helping me as much as I thought it would," she said.

"Why not?"

"I never thought I would see it happen for one of my sons..."

A guard tapped his stick against the bars on the cell next to mine and Mama and I both looked over at him, he pointed at his watch and then jerked his head towards the door.

Mama nodded and looked back at me, "I'm going to miss you," she said.

I nodded and bowed my head, Mama reached through the bars one last time and placed her hand on top of my head before stepping back and wrapping her scarf around herself tightly. She followed the guard towards the exit, keeping her eyes on me the entire time. I could see the tears sliding down her face. Mama and I kept our eyes on each other until the guards helped her through the door and shut it behind her.

I am thankful for the fact that I got to see everyone before this, especially Mama, who I didn't think I would ever get to see again. I hope my family can forgive me for all the pain and trouble I've caused them over the years. I hope Nargis can forgive me for ruining our chances at a life together. I hope she marries someone who is kind and caring and good to her. I hope Yaqeen and bhabi have many more happy, healthy children. I hope they both grow old and grey together. I hope Mama lives to be an extremely old woman, a great grandmother perhaps. There is much more that I would like to say, but Nassir Uncle is standing outside my cell now, waiting to take me through the other door. I am not afraid, I have no reason to be. I know that I am innocent. I have to end this for now, I'll have to write more some other time.

The Kings of the World

A lot of people make not crying when you get hit look easy, I never found it to be very easy. That's why I had to pretend that I was trying to catch my breath instead of holding back tears when Abdullah hit me.

"Come on, ass. Get up," he said.

I swallowed hard and looked up at him, he was grinning but in a very mean and cruel way.

"Are you going to cry?" he asked with a laugh, his friends standing behind him laughed too.

"No," I said quietly as I got up and brushed some of the dirt off of my pants.

Abdullah stopped laughing and scowled at me, "I didn't say you could get up," he said before grabbing my tie and pulling on it hard, causing me to stumble forward and almost fall down again.

I straightened up again, grabbed his hands, and tried to wrench my tie out of his grasp, "Let it go," I pleaded, "you'll rip it!"

He laughed in my face (his breath smelled like cigarettes and old mints) and said, "Make me."

"Let him go Abdullah," said a voice from behind me.

Abdullah and his friends stopped laughing and they all stared at the person standing behind me with scowls on their faces. And a bit of fear as well. I turned my head a little to look and saw Zoe standing behind me, he was smoking a cigarette and casually flicking a lighter in one hand.

"Are you deaf?" he asked.

Abdullah sneered, "What'll you do if I don't?"

Zoe smiled, "I'll pin you down and burn your eyes out," he said, holding up the lighter.

The sneer was gone and now Abdullah was eyeing the lighter in Zoe's hand apprehensively, he let go of my tie and took a few steps back.

"You think you're cool smoking and walking around flicking that lighter?" he asked quietly, trying to keep his voice steady.

"No. I don't think smoking makes me cool," said Zoe calmly, "You and all of your wives over there do it too, can't be that cool."

Some of the boys standing behind Abdullah cracked their knuckles menacingly, but none of them made a move. Abdullah glared at Zoe for a few seconds before motioning to his friends, "Come on, let's go," he said. As they were all walking away Abdullah turned back to look at me and said, "He won't always be around to protect you."

"Don't be so sure!" Zoe said with a wave and a smile.

Abdullah clenched his jaw but said nothing, instead he turned around and kept on walking.

Once the boys were gone, the two of us turned and started walking in the opposite direction. Zoe looked at me and asked, "Are you okay?"

I nodded.

"You're lying. Did you cry?"

I felt my face go red and I reached up and hastily brushed away at the corners of my eyes.

"It's okay," he said, "but what were you thinking? Why would you take one of the alleyways? You know that's where they hang around."

"It was a shortcut home," I said with a shrug.

Zoe shook his head, "Did you say anything to him?"

"No. Not at first. He was sitting on the wall smoking with his friends and when he saw me, they all jumped down and blocked my way and he asked me why I dressed like an ass. So I said that someone who cuts the sleeves off of their school shirts doesn't have much of a right to call anyone an ass."

Zoe let out a bark of laughter and shook his head again, "Idiot."

Abdullah cut the sleeves off of all of his school shirts to show off his muscles and everyone made fun of him behind his back for it, but nobody ever did it to his face because they were all scared of him. Nobody but Zoe. And me now I guess.

"Where'd he hit you?" Zoe asked.

I gestured at my stomach and he frowned, "You've gotta learn how to fight," he said.

"I don't know how."

"Yes you do. Everyone does. It's almost like a human instinct to know how to hit things, all you need is to learn how to use that instinct."

I didn't want to argue with that logic.

"Why's it so important that I learn how to use my instinct? I've got you," I said with a grin.

Even though he tried to make a serious face, I could see a smirk tugging at the corner of Zoe's mouth, "You won't always," he said, "I'm three years older than you, I could be gone from here in a few weeks for all you know."

"Where would you go?" I asked.

He shrugged, "Don't know. University? Maybe Dubai or America."

"I don't think you can get to Dubai or America on your bike Zoe."

Zoe chuckled and nudged me with elbow, "That's big talk coming from someone who can't even ride yet."

"Abba says he won't teach me until I'm sixteen, two more years," I said bitterly.

"Why wait for him to teach you? I taught myself when I was eleven! Just do what I did, sneak out when he's asleep, get on his bike, and just go."

"How mad was your father when he caught you?" I asked.

Zoe looked over at me and I saw that he was grinning, "I couldn't feel anything for two days when he was done with me, but still, I learned didn't I?"

I laughed and then went quiet for a few seconds.

"I don't think I could do that though," I said when I finally spoke again, "I mean I don't think I could learn like that. I'm not like you."

He threw his cigarette on the ground and crushed it with his foot as he walked, "What do you mean 'not like me?'" he asked.

I shrugged, "I don't know...you can do things like that, you can stand up to Abdullah and his friends without any help, you can fight them if you have to without any help, you can get on a bike when you're eleven and just go and learn what to do. I can't do things like that."

"Oh shut up. Don't start with that excuse, you can do whatever I can do and you could probably do it better. You're just too afraid, you give up on yourself before you try anything. Besides, you're smarter than I am. You don't see me complaining."

"Only in school," I said, "And that's only because you barely show up and when you do, you don't do any work."

As I spoke, Zoe fished another cigarette out of his pocket, stuck it between his lips, and lit it. After exhaling a cloud of smoke, he chuckled.

"What's so funny?" I asked.

He shook his head at me, "I can't do the work. It goes against my nature."

"What do you mean?"

He shook his head again and said, "I'll explain some other time. Anyway, we're here."

We both stopped walking and stared across the street at the front gates of my house.

"How much does that place cost your parents?" he asked.

I shrugged, "I don't know. Amma grew up in that house and we moved into it two years ago when her parents died because she was their only kid and wanted to be back home, I've never asked how much it costs."

"Yeah...you've told me but damn that's a beautiful looking house..." Zoe shook his head and turned his attention back to me with a serious look on his face, "You got lucky this time, but from now on, avoid all of the 'shortcuts' you know about, got it? I can't always show up when you need me."

I nodded my head.

"No. I mean it, I'm serious. Do you promise?"

At this, I grinned before saying, "I promise."

Zoe frowned, "What's so funny?"

"Big, dangerous Zoe is all caring," I teased.

He laughed and nudged me with his elbow again.

"I should get going," he said once he'd stopped laughing.

"Are you sure? Do you want to come inside and hang out for a while?"

He shook his head, "No. Not today. *Churail* will throw a fit," he said.

"I can't believe you call her that."

"Not to her face, to her face I call her Ina but she hates that too. Says I should call her 'mother,' as if she deserves that."

"Does your dad know about anything yet?" I asked quietly.

Zoe's face darkened and I saw him clench his jaw, "No. Nothing. And he wouldn't believe it anyway," he snapped.

I opened my mouth to apologize but Zoe cut me off, "Sorry. I just don't like talking about him. Or her."

"I know. I'm sorry for asking."

His face relaxed and he sighed before tossing his cigarette on the ground and putting it out with his foot again.

"Why do you want me to come over so much lately?" he asked suspiciously.

"Amma wants to meet you, she keeps saying I should invite you for some chai or for dinner or something. I keep putting it off but she doesn't forget about it."

"Why is she so desperate to meet me?"

"Wants to make sure you're not a bad influence, I think," I said with a shrug, "You're the only friend I always hang around with. It's been two years and she's never met you. She's probably going to start following me around just to meet you soon."

Zoe stared at me for a few seconds with an odd expression on his face, but right before I could ask him what he was staring at, his face broke into a grin, "I'll be sure to come over soon then!"

He started walking backwards in the opposite direction and as he was leaving I asked, "Will you be in school tomorrow?"

"Maybe!" he called back.

I shook my head and smiled at him before turning around and running across the street to my house.

Before going inside, I made sure to tuck my school shirt back in, straighten out my tie, and brush any dirt that I could see off of my clothes. After fixing my clothes I rubbed my eyes hard with the backs of my hands to try to wipe away any signs that showed that I had been crying, and I reached up and brushed my hair back with my hands. Using the large, gold, square shaped nameplates on the gates, I checked my reflection one last time to make sure that no signs of my encounter with Abdullah were showing before I reached out and rang the bell.

I pushed what happened that afternoon to the back of my mind for the rest of the day. I took a nap, ate dinner with Amma (Abba had to work all night), did my homework, and went to bed. The next day at school I didn't see Zoe. Which was normal, he was an upperclassman and, other than occasionally in the halls in between classes and sometimes at lunch, I didn't see him much anyway. But when he wasn't there at the end of the day I figured he had skipped school. Which was also normal for Zoe. In fact it was a bit of a joke amongst the students and teachers at our school. Once or twice every month Zoe wouldn't show up for a couple of days, sometimes a whole week, and then he'd be back in class like nothing happened. He never talked about where he went and teachers never pressed him too much. I think the teachers saw him as a lazy and unmotivated slacker and maybe that's why they didn't press him much. And if that is what they thought, he didn't do much to prove them wrong. Zoe wasn't stupid, he would fail for most of the year and then at the very end of the term he'd pull his grades up just enough to pass the year. Some students came up with their own theories about where he went and those theories eventually turned into rumors. He was a part of a gang, or he went from Karachi to Multan on the days that he disappeared to race bikes and gamble with grown men in the city, or he went around the city at night and competed in fights in back alleys for money and that's why he had bruises on his face whenever he showed up again, and so on. All of these rumors came with whispers, "he's dangerous!" "look at his long hair, he grows it out so he looks older," "he thinks he's so tough, pah! I'll bet I could knock him out," "See the ring he wears? I saw him steal it from the jeweler's shop at the mall, he never gets caught," etc. Those were mainly all from the other boys in the school. The girls whispered too, but they didn't care much for the rumors about how dangerous he was, they liked him. It wasn't hard to see why, Zoe was very good looking. He had long, dark brown hair that he sometimes tied back in a ponytail and dark brown eyes that always locked onto yours when you spoke to him, and he was tall and muscular too. But the physical stuff wasn't the main thing. He was *nice*. Most boys acted a certain way and tried to be impressive with their acts, but Zoe was always light and joking and polite. He wasn't really bad to anyone, he just took pleasure in teasing everyone he came across. The only people he disliked were people like Abdullah and his gang.

But despite all of the whispers and rumors and stories that flew around, from girls and boys alike, I was the only person who knew the real reason for Zoe's constant vanishing. Whenever his father's second wife got particularly rough with him, Zoe would skip school until he healed up a little. He let people carry on with their theories, but that was the real reason. I don't think his father ever noticed, if he did then he didn't ever do anything about it. Although I sometimes wished I had his looks or his confidence, I wouldn't want Zoe's life. I wouldn't want any part of it at all.

On Thursday, his third day of being gone, I got a call from Zoe. I'd just gotten home from school and I was in my room getting my phone out of my bag when it rang in my hand.

"Hello?" I said.

On the other end, Zoe was doing his best imitation of an old woman, "Hello sahib, I was wondering if you would like to join me for some chai?"

"If you're trying to do a joke phone call, you should call someone who doesn't have caller ID."

Zoe kept up the act, "Yes sahib. Of course sahib. But I'm not joking sahib. I'm just a little old lady who wants some company."

I couldn't help but laugh a little and then I asked, "Where are you?"

"Old Khan's roof," he said in his normal voice.

"What? What're you doing there?"

"He lets me stay here. But that's not important, are you going to come or not?"

"Right now?" I asked, wondering how I would explain to Amma where I was going.

"No, not right now. Later tonight, when your parents go to sleep. You know where it is right?"

"Everyone knows where it is Zoe."

"Good. Oh and bring some *shakkar* when you come."

"Why?" I asked.

"Because I don't have any and we'll both have to drink bitter chai if you don't, that's why. Oh and bring some tea bags too."

"If I'm bringing the tea bags and the *shakkar*, what does that leave for you to bring?"

"Water," he said simply, "And the flame we'll be boiling the water over. And the food. Are you satisfied sahib?" he switched to the quaky, old woman's voice again.

"Fine. But I won't be able to leave until after nine, if Abba's coming home, he'll be home by then. If he doesn't, Amma will go to bed and then I can sneak out."

"Alright," he said and we exchanged goodbyes, and then I hung up.

That night, after Amma had made her cup of chai after dinner, I snuck into the kitchen while she was watching T.V. and grabbed the jar of *shakkar* and a handful of tea bags, ran to my room, and stuffed them into my bag. I stayed in my room, finished my homework, and then just laid around waiting for

Amma to go to bed. Around nine fifteen, after Abba still hadn't come home, I heard Amma come upstairs and go into her room. Twenty minutes late I heard her bedroom door shut, I waited a few minutes, and when she didn't come out again, I grabbed my bag, opened my window, climbed out, lowered myself down halfway, and then dropped down into the garden. When I got to our gate, I pushed it open a quarter of the way as slowly as I could and then I squeezed myself through sideways, making sure to push it closed behind me. There wasn't much noise coming from the houses in our neighborhood, but the streets were just as busy at night as they were during the day. All of the little boutiques had been closed, but there were still vendors going up and down the street, dragging their wagons full of kabobs and sweets and drinks behind them, calling out to people as they drove or walked by. The all night corner market still had people going in and out of it, mainly grown men now but a few kids too. As I walked by, I felt myself starting to grin, I had never been out this late before. At least not by myself, and definitely not on foot.

When the guards standing by the fence to our neighborhood saw me coming, they looked a little confused, but none of them said anything and they let me through.

"*Shukriya!*" I called back to one of them and he nodded and gave a little wave in response.

Now, instead of turning left and going up the main road I ran across to the apartment buildings on the other side of the street and ducked into one of the side alleyways. If I walked along the main road it would take me thirty minutes or so to get to Old Khan's house because I'd be spending most of my time dodging cars and trying not to bump into vendors. Cutting through the neighborhoods would only take me twenty minutes or so. Everyone in our part of Karachi knew where Old Khan lived I think and that's because Old Khan had lived in the same place for over thirty years. Although, he probably wasn't *Old* Khan back then. He had fought in a war, but nobody ever knew which one and you couldn't ask him because he wouldn't tell you. In fact, I don't think he ever spoke to anyone. I'd only seen him a couple of times, he was a stern looking old man with scars everywhere. Scars on the backs of his hands, his face, his arms, all over. When Ammi had lived in our house as a girl, she had known him too. She told me that he'd been a sweet old man and that he wasn't as scarred back then, but I don't think she remembered him correctly. I can't imagine him ever not having scars.

While I was walking I couldn't help noticing how hot it was, I could feel sweat pouring down the back of my neck and I felt little drops of sweat falling off of my nose every few seconds. I didn't know what Zoe was thinking, wanting to drink chai on a night when it was so hot out, but then, I didn't know what Zoe was thinking half the time anyway. By the time I reached Old Khan's neighborhood I was sweating all over and feeling a little dizzy. His house was the one at the end of the street, the largest house there, but also the plainest looking. A large white building, the two front windows had grills in front of them and the small balcony on the second floor of the house had nothing on it except for a broomstick in the corner. There was no gate in front of his house, which wasn't unusual since there were a few other houses on the street that didn't have gates, but those houses had potted plants placed out in front, or chairs, or little tables, some even had beds. But not his. There was nothing in front of his house but the cracked cement ground leading onto the dirt covered sidewalk and the only thing you could see outside as you got close to the house was a large generator sitting quietly near the right side of the house. There was a light on in one of the windows and as I got closer I thought about pulling out my phone and texting Zoe to tell him that I was outside, but before I could do that the front door swung open and Old Khan stepped out.

He was holding a little wooden walking stick in his left hand and was hunched over a little, but even like that, he was a large man. Over six feet tall at least, and broad shouldered. He had on a light blue *salwar kameez* that looked old and faded, the top had a few rips in it along the sleeves, which were rolled up to his elbows. On his head he was wearing a brown *pakol* and his grey hair was sticking out from under the sides. He didn't say anything, he just stood there staring at me as I nervously approached him and asked if I could see Zoe. When he didn't say anything, I asked again, Old Khan cocked his head to the side and kept staring at me. I was thinking, again, about texting Zoe again, but at that moment, he came running out the front door right behind Old Khan.

"Khan-ji!" he yelled and Old Khan turned to look at him. He said something to Zoe in a language I didn't recognize right away, he gestured at me with his hand while he spoke and Zoe grinned and responded in the same language. And I suddenly realized what it was, they were both speaking Pashto. Old Khan was nodding his head and mumbling something to Zoe and Zoe was smiling and pointing up while he talked. After a couple of minutes of this, Old Khan turned back to me and jerked his head towards the door, when I didn't move, he motioned to me to come in with his hand and Zoe said, "Come on! We're going up!"

I walked forward as Old Khan turned around and went back inside, Zoe grabbed me by the arm and dragged me in through the front door. There was the kitchen as soon as we walked in, with a little refrigerator in the corner and a small dining table on the other side, Old Khan was bending low over the table, picking up some of the remaining dishes. On the far side of the kitchen, right by the counter, there was a set of stairs leading up and that's what Zoe pulled me to. I went up the stairs behind him, turned right, started up a second flight of stairs and I immediately felt as if somebody had put a hot, stuffy hand over my mouth and nose, making it nearly impossible for me to breathe. It was so hot in this little stairwell, I was sure that if I were to sit down on the steps for a few seconds, I would die of suffocation. Zoe was tugging on my arm even though I was slowing down to try and breathe.

"Come on," he mumbled, sounding a little strained himself, "It'll be better once we get to the roof, only two more flights!"

And then he started bounding up the steps, skipping every other step as he went and since he was still holding onto me, I had to do my best to keep up and not fall flat on my face as we went. Just when I was starting to think that the stairs would never end we reached a door and Zoe pushed it open all the way with his free hand and pulled me out onto the rooftop with him. As soon as I stepped out, the heat and stuffiness of the staircase seemed like a distant bad dream. The wind was blowing up here and I could feel every bit of it, I took a deep breath and almost sighed out loud with contentment. It wasn't the cleanest air, I could still smell a hint of the city on the wind, but it was as good as anyone in the city could get. I looked around and saw a gas hose leading out from a little shed in one corner of the rooftop and right above the nozzle, which was blasting out a small and steady blue flame, was a small grill and on top of that grill was a little tin pot. I could hear bubbling coming from inside the pot and I didn't have to get a closer look at it to guess what it was.

"The water?" I asked Zoe.

"That's right, did you bring the tea bags and *shakkar*?"

I swung my bag off of my shoulders, opened it up, reached inside and pulled out the tea bags and the jar of *shakkar* and handed it all to him.

He grinned and walked over to where the pot was and sat down next to it before carefully dropping all of the tea bags inside. There was a loud hiss and the bubbling got louder and Zoe waited a few seconds before opening the jar of *shakkar* and scooping a bunch of it into the pot as well. After doing that, he reached over to the side and twisted the knob next to the nozzle to turn the heat down a bit, "It'll be ready soon," he said as he sat back and brought his knees up into his chest.

I nodded and walked over to the edge of the rooftop, when I looked down I could see up and down the entire length of the neighborhood as well as way beyond the gates, back up towards the highway in the direction that I'd come from. The highway was still flooded with cars, motorbikes, and people, and all of the sound was carried up to us by the wind. But if I took a couple of steps back, I wouldn't be able to see any of the lights. Just a dim glow rising up from the streets beyond, but down below in the neighborhood it was silent and dark except for the light from the guards' station. I stepped back from the edge and took another deep breath and this time a small sigh did escape me, and I heard Zoe laugh.

"Good, isn't it?" he asked.

I turned around to look at him, "What?"

"The air," he was turning off the gas now and pulling a pair of small silver tongs out of his pocket, "The wind blowing and everything, the fresh air. Well, as fresh as it'll get." I nodded, but he didn't notice, "The wind blows here from Seaview, only a few people get to feel it, everybody down there can't," he looked up at me then and raised an eyebrow, "Are you just going to stand there Amir or are you going to help?"

"What do you want me to do?" I asked.

"Go over to that table over there," he jerked his head to the right, "And grab those two mugs and that paper bag."

I went over to an old wooden table that was sitting against the wall on the side of the rooftop and grabbed two chipped mugs that were resting upside down on the table and a paper bag that was slightly warm to the touch. I carried it all back over to Zoe and handed him the cups and set the bag down beside him.

"What's in the bag?" I asked.

"Eclairs," he mumbled without looking up at me as he was now lifting the pot up off of the grill carefully with the tongs and pouring hot chai out through a tiny strainer he held with his other hand into one of the cups on the ground in front of him. Once he was finished pouring in one, he moved the strainer up over the other cup and poured chai into that one as well. When he finished pouring, he sighed and set the pot carefully back down on the grill before covering it with the lid. He turned to look up at me and said, "Not a drop on the ground."

"Good job. But aren't you forgetting something?" I asked.

"Uhh...no?"

"Milk?"

"Shit!" Zoe sprang up to his feet, "I'm such an idiot! Hold on, stay here, I'll run down and get some," and he bolted to the door and ran back down the stairs while I laughed. While I was waiting for him to come back up, I had a chance to completely take in my surroundings. The rooftop was big, somebody could have a party for at least fifty people up on the roof and still have some room left over. There was the shed in one corner, its door was open to allow the gas hose to come out and I noticed that there was another generator plugged in inside as well, this one was much bigger than the one downstairs. In the corner opposite the shed, there was a pile of chipped and broken bricks along with a bunch of wooden planks leaned up against the wall. Amongst the bricks were some old and rusty nails along with a spade that was broken in half. The table was next to the pile of bricks and to my left, there was nothing but a few potted plants along the sidewall and a small bedframe with multicolored bamboo weaving wound inside the frame in place of a mattress. I went up to the frame and pushed down on it gently with my hand, it didn't give much, and I was just wondering who would sleep on something that sturdy when Zoe shoved the door open and came out carrying a small jug of milk in his hands.

"Admiring my bed?" he asked.

"You sleep on this?" I asked with mild surprise.

"Yup. Whenever I'm here, I sleep up here on the roof on that frame. It's more comfortable than it looks, trust me," he explained as he stooped down and carefully poured milk into both of the cups, "By the way, Khan-ji says he's sorry if he scared you, he just didn't know who you were. Thought you were one of the boys who throws eggs at his house sometimes."

A question suddenly sprang into my mind, "Where'd you learn to speak Pashto?!" I blurted out. Zoe didn't answer right away, instead he patted on the ground next to him and when I sat down, he handed me one of the cups and pulled his knees into his chest again. After blowing on his chai and taking a small sip, he said, "Amma taught me. When I was younger. My grandfather was Pathan and she learned it from him and when I was little she taught me."

"You never told me that," I said.

He smiled and shrugged, "You never asked. Now drink your chai before it gets cold."

I lifted the cup up to my lips and took a sip. Warmth immediately spread from the tips of my fingers down to my toes and the sweetest taste I'd ever tasted spread across my tongue, immediately, I felt myself wake up a bit more and I took another sip.

I shook my head a few times, "Woah."

"Good isn't it?" Zoe was grinning, "That'll wake you up. I'm the best at making chai," he said proudly.

"You should leave school and open up your own shop somewhere in the city," I leaned back a little on my elbows and took another sip.

"Or in the mountains. Or some small village. I could call it, 'Strong and Sweet,' just like me," he laughed and grabbed the bag of eclairs, putting it in between the both of us.

"Don't get ahead of yourself," I chuckled as I pulled out an éclair, "Where'd you get these?"

"Blue Ribbon," he reached into the bag and pulled one out for himself, "Had some money left over from the summer, thought it might be nice to have something to eat with the chai."

I took a big bite of the éclair and immediately realized that, due to the combined flavors of the chai and the éclair, the inside of my mouth had never been sweeter. And I had no problem with that.

For the next few minutes, the only sounds were the sounds of Zoe and I chewing, sipping our chai, the dulled noises from the highway, and the quiet whistling of the wind. We both helped ourselves to more eclairs from the bag, and more chai from the tin pot. Finally, we both set our cups down and leaned back on our elbows, me with my legs stretched out in front of me, and Zoe with his legs crossed, his head tilted back, and his eyes closed. His hair fell back away from his face when he sat like that and I noticed in the dim light that he had something above his left eye.

"Zoe..."

His eyes snapped open and he sat up again, "Hold on," and he reached into his pocket and pulled something out, he reached out with his other hand and very slowly turned the gas nozzle a little bit. The small blue flame shot up and he cupped his hands over it for a second and then immediately pulled them away. He brought the hand up to his face and when I saw the floating ember, I realized that the thing he'd pulled out had been a cigarette.

"Can't you use a lighter you maniac?" I asked.

He turned the gas off again and laughed, "I left it downstairs, I could go down and get it...but that's all the way downstairs."

I shook my head and then remembered what I wanted to ask, "Zoe?"

"Hmm?"

"What's that above your eye?"

No response.

"Zoe?"

"Cut," he grunted.

"What?"

He sighed and moved over closer to me so that he and I were sitting face to face, he held the cigarette in one hand and reached up with the other one to push a lock of hair away from his face and I finally got a good and up close look at him. There were two white bandage strips taped down over a cut going through the middle of his left eyebrow and up his forehead. The eye was swollen just a little bit and there was some bruising around it. And there was another cut across the bridge of his nose, not deep, and in the process of healing, but even in the dim light I could tell that that part of his nose was slightly swollen as well. When I didn't say anything he turned his body to face away from me again and tilted his head back to blow smoke upwards.

"What happened?" I finally asked.

"*Churail* tried to do my make up with a rolling pin," he said simply.

"Why? What'd you do?"

He shrugged and gave me a sidelong glance along with a smirk, "I don't know. Probably said something. I say a lot to her. She's bound to catch some of it, as stupid as she may be." He was grinning but I thought I could hear a hint of bitterness in his voice when he talked about his stepmother.

"I'm sorry Zoe."

"Don't be. Besides, girls like scars, right?"

I laughed, "Some do maybe?"

He took another drag from his cigarette and smiled, "I'll have to find those some then."

"Zoe, why don't you tell your-"

"He doesn't want to hear it," Zoe snapped, "In his eyes, it's my fault anyway. Says she's got a right to do it, she's my new mom now. And whenever he says that, I remind him that my actual mom is still laying in bed upstairs, not dead yet like he's probably hoping. And then he has a shot at me too. There's no point."

We were both silent for a moment and then he got up and walked over to the wall and flicked his cigarette off over the edge. When he came back and sat down, he pulled his knees into his chest again, "I'm sorry. I wasn't trying to attack you, I just hate thinking about them. About her."

I stayed quiet. Zoe didn't talk about things at home much, all I knew was that he hated his step mother and that she regularly used him as a punching bag.

"I hate having to skip school because of her," he said, "I don't *always* skip cause of her, but I mean, I hate having to do it when she goes at me."

"Do you always come here?" I asked.

He shook his head, "No. Not always. A lot of the time I do. I drop in and out, Khan-ji takes care of me. He's the one who bandaged this up," he pointed up at his eye, "And put a rub on my nose. Lets me spend the night up here, gives me food. I don't know. He takes care of me as good as Amma did before she got sick. Or Abba before he married *her*."

"How long have you known him anyway?"

"Few years," he said with a shrug, "He caught me trying to steal his bike."

"He *what*?!"

"Well, not really 'steal,' I was going to bring it back after I took it out for a ride. He's got a big, old chopper in the back of the house. And I was walking through the neighborhood after visiting some of the shops around the corner, he had it parked out front, I don't know why. He might've been working on it or something, maybe cleaning it. But it was just sitting right there, so I went over and sat on it and as soon as I started it, he grabbed me by the ear and pulled me off." Zoe grinned, "He cursed at me in Pashto, so I responded in Pashto and he was surprised by that."

"Why the surprise? Pashto isn't uncommon."

"I know, but he's the only one who speaks it in this neighborhood. He took me inside and we talked then, I swore to him that I'd planned on bringing his bike back. I don't know. He seemed very...amused, once he stopped being mad. Like I was telling him a joke or something. Then I started coming here once a week. And I showed up here the first time *churail* beat me up, a little while after Abba married her. I've been coming here since."

"Does he talk to you?"

"What do you mean by that? Of course he talks to me, what else would he do?"

"No, but, does he tell you about himself?"

"Yes. He's been in Pakistan since he was seventeen, his family moved here from Afghanistan when things started getting tense, back in 1978. And then the Afghan and Soviet war started right after that and that was the first war he fought in. He wasn't even eighteen when it started. Fought during Siachen too. He's fought a lot. He had a wife too, she got cancer a little while after they got married and died. He's kept to himself since then."

"Wow..." I said quietly.

"What?"

"All of that. I mean, he told you all of that. I don't think he talks to anyone, I don't think anyone knows any of that about him."

"Well nobody ever asks him. Or talks to him. Everyone just thinks he's some mad old veteran with a lot of scars." Zoe stretched his legs out and laid on his side, propping his head up with one hand to be able look at me as he spoke.

"How come you never told me any of it? About visiting him and everything?"

"You never asked Amir."

"Ass," I muttered and we both laughed.

Once the laughter died down, it was quiet again. I was staring out over the edge of the rooftop, not really looking at anything. And even though I could feel Zoe's eyes staring in my direction, I knew that he wasn't looking at me either.

After a couple minutes, he broke the silence in a soft voice, "What do you want to do?" he asked.

I turned to look at him, "Huh?"

Zoe's eyes were pointing down and he was moving his finger in a circle on the cement rooftop, making a quiet scratching nose as he spoke, "What do you want to do?" he repeated.

"How do you mean?" I asked.

He looked up at me and his finger stopped moving, "Ten years from now, what do you want to be doing? Where do you want to be? What kind of people do you want to be with? What do you want to do?"

"I...I don't know," I spoke very slowly, "I haven't thought about it that much. Sometimes I do, and I think that I'd want to be an engineer. Probably here in Karachi, so I'm close to home. Or maybe in Islamabad. Or Lahore. But I'm not sure. Because that can change can't it? Ten years is a long time."

"That's right, that's good. That you know that, that it can change and that it's not permanent or anything."

He went quiet again so I spoke up, "Why'd you ask me that?"

"We've been friends for years and I feel like I should know that about my friend. My only friend, if you think about it."

"That's not true!"

He raised an eyebrow at me and grinned, "Isn't it? Name one person that I hang around with other than you. Anyone."

I thought about it, wracked my brains trying to pull up an image of Zoe with anyone from school, "Uhmmm..."

"Go on."

"I can't think of anyone," I finally admitted.

Zoe laughed, "That's cause there isn't anyone, idiot. It's just you. That's it. And I don't know why, since you're younger than I am and I don't know, smarter than I am."

"We went over this the other day! Not in everything, I'm smarter than you in some things only. And you're much smarter than me in other things. Everyone's like that."

He didn't say anything to that, instead he chewed on his bottom lip for a few seconds and then looked up at me again, "Do you want to know what I want to do?"

I nodded.

"I want to go."

"Go where?" I asked.

"I just want to go. Go. I don't know. I haven't decided. But away from here. Anywhere. Everywhere. Maybe go to Aisha in

Australia and see what it's like there. And then to Europe, I can to go Paris, England, Germany, Belgium. And then I can to go to China, Japan, Russia, and Greenland. And then Dubai, and Egypt, Turkey, America. And then after all of that I can come back to Pakistan."

"You want to travel all over the world?"

"No, no... I don't know. Yes and no. I'd like to, I'd like to see a lot and be everywhere at once. But I want to go, just go and see it all, and be there, and experience it. And then, once I have, I want to come back and go to one of the villages. Somewhere near the mountains maybe. And I want to live there. In a little cottage, where I can chop firewood, and get water from the ice glaciers, and walk around and see everything and just be someplace quiet. Where there isn't much to worry about."

"What about your family?"

Anger flashed across his face, "What about them?" he spat, but then his expression softened, "I'd take Amma with me," he said quietly, "Maybe not everywhere, but away from here. Maybe to Aisha, or maybe just...I don't know. But I'd take her with me." He went quiet again and for a second I thought he'd gotten lost in thought, but then he spoke again, "It's so beautiful everywhere. There's beauty all over. Allah put it all around us, and I want to feel it. I want to feel it in my bones. Something good and pure like that. I'm sick of being here. I don't even have to go everywhere actually, if I could just go with that village idea. I'd be okay."

I brought my legs in to cross them and cleared my throat before asking, "Why that one? I mean, what's so wonderful about being in a little village?"

"It's...something smaller, more manageable, simpler. That matters to me. I know some people love it here in the city, and they'd love cities all over the world too, but there's too much here. Too much for me. And it suffocates me. When I come up here, come up here on this rooftop I mean, and I take a deep breath and I feel that wind running over me, it's like I'm breathing for the first time. I don't know, I can't explain it very well. But being up here is the closest I get to being away from it all, and then whenever I eventually go back down, I'm back in it. Back in everything. But I want to feel that all the time. The way I do when I come up here I mean." He rolled over onto his back and put both hands behind his head, "I want to be able to lay like this and stare up at the stars and not have to hear anything except for the night sounds. I want that kind of quiet, I want to feel like it's swallowing me whole, I wish I could lose myself in that. Wouldn't you like something like that? Not forever, but wouldn't you like to experience that at least once?"

"The way you describe it...yes, I would. Probably not for the rest of my life, but for a little while," I said softly with a smile.

He didn't see the smile, since he'd closed his eyes, but he kept talking, "I'm not completely sure I'd like it forever either, maybe I'd eventually want to come back to someplace like this. But I do need it for a bit of time, I need to get away from stuff like this. Maybe I'd even have a wife. Maybe."

I grinned, "What kind of wife? Like the girls from school?"

Zoe laughed without opening his eyes, "No. Someone I can talk to. I don't care what she looks like or how much money her family has or anything like that. I want to be able to talk to someone, and have them be able to talk to me. It'd be nice if she was really pretty, but when we're both sixty years old and hunched over and wrinkly and half blind, what the hell will I care who's pretty or not?"

"Yeah," I agreed. I didn't know what else to say, but Zoe didn't seem to mind.

"I'm sorry Amir. I've been talking this whole time. But sometimes when I'm feeling this way, I have to tell someone. And there's usually no one around, I can't talk to Khan-ji about all of this stuff. Some stuff, yeah. But not everything."

"I don't mind!" I said quickly, "I really don't mind. You're my friend Zoe. You stand up for me, you protect me. I just don't always know what to say to things all the time."

Zoe opened one eye to look at me, "Tell me about you then. How you feel."

"Huh?"

"I'm upset because I feel trapped and because of what I go through at home, what about you? What upsets you?"

"Uh...," I knew what upset me, but I didn't want to tell Zoe about it, it seemed small next to what he went through at home, and yet..."I guess, Abba."

"What about him?"

"He's not around," I said with a shrug, "I understand why," I hastily added, "I do. I mean, the reason we can afford Ammi's old house and have a good life is because, you know, he's the commissioner. People respect him, he's great at his job, and he worked hard to get there. But he's never there. Or here. I mean, he's never in my life." I paused to wait for him to say something, when he didn't, I continued, "I know he's proud whenever something happens, he's really proud. But I just wish I could see that on his face sometimes, in person. I wish I didn't have to tell him nearly everything over the phone and just guess how he's feeling by his voice, which always sounds tired anyway. And it's not just me, I know Ammi tries to act like she's not bothered by it, but she is too. Both of us are lonely, but we don't talk about it. I don't know why, but I can't talk to her about it. And I don't think that she *wants* to talk to me about it."

"You should talk to her about it."

"Why?"

"It's hard to explain, she won't come to you, but she wants to talk about it. And you're the only one who would understand her, just like she's the only one who would understand you," he explained.

"Did you ever talk to your mom about things? Before she...well..." my voice trailed off.

No response.

"I'm sorry, I shouldn't-"

"We did," he interrupted. "All of the time." I stared at him and he continued, "I remember, she would make chai for both of us when I came home from school, and we would sit in the kitchen and talk. And then she'd read me poetry, Rumi, Hafez, Meera..." his voice broke a little and, even though I couldn't see it in the dark, I was certain that he was crying. And sure enough, I saw him reach up and wipe his eyes with the back of his hand.

We were both went silent again, but this time it seemed quieter. Even the noise that had been rising up from beyond the rooftop seemed distant now, as if someone had turned the volume down. The wind had picked up speed, and a gust of it hit me in the face, blowing my hair back and wrapping itself around me. I suddenly became aware of how relaxed I felt and I was afraid that if I closed my eyes, I'd wind up falling asleep for a week.

"There it is," he said.

"What?"

"You felt it too. That feeling." He sprang up to his feet and walked over to the wall again, this time he swung his legs over and sat on the edge, staring out past the dark of the neighborhood. "The one that I feel all the time when I take my bike out on the N-5 at night, when it's two in the morning and there aren't that many other cars out. I'll be riding along and that wind hits me, I feel like I can go on forever. Go on in that moment forever. And the only stoplight that I'll hit is the sun crawling up over the horizon and blasting me in the face. It's like another planet or something..."

He turned back around to face me while he sat, "Thank you," he said quietly, "Thanks for coming. And for listening." He got down off the wall and stared at me, and I stared back. For a split second, I thought he was going to say something else too, but instead, he just reached up and stretched.

"Do you want to stay here tonight?" he asked.

"What?" I didn't know what time it was, "Oh," I pulled my phone out of my pocket and checked, it was nearly three in the morning. "Oh!" I said again, I quickly stood up and brushed off the seat of my pants.

"What's wrong?"

"Zoe, I've got to go. If I'm not home before Fajr, Ammi will wake up and see that I'm gone.'

He stared at me with a funny expression on his face and then his face split into a wide grin, "Right. Well then, another time maybe."

I began walking towards the door leading downstairs and he walked with me, "Are you going to be okay?" I asked.

"I'll be fine. I think I'll stretch out and go to sleep for the night."

"Will you be able to after all the chai we drank?"

Zoe smirked, "I can go to sleep no matter what."

I laughed, "Alright. Will I see you in school later?"

"Maybe, maybe tomorrow. Maybe never again," he said with a shrug.

"Zoe!"

"I'm joking. If I don't go today, I'll be there for sure tomorrow," he said as he held the door open for me.

"Promise?"

He nodded his head absentmindedly, "Yes, yes, I promise."

"Alright, well, I'll see you soon then."

"You will," he said with a smile.

We shook hands with one another and I stepped into the stuffy, hot stairwell, pulling the door to the rooftop shut behind me. I made my way down the stairs and into the now darkened kitchen. The only source of light was a small gas lamp in the corner.

"Khan-ji must've gone to bed," I thought to myself as I made my way over to the door and stepped outside. Part of me wanted to run back into the house, run back up those stairs, and spend the rest of the night up on that roof. In case Zoe wanted to talk some more, but I knew I couldn't. And anyway, he'd be okay. If there was anything worth talking about, he'd text, or call, or just tell me about it when he came back to school. It wasn't very reassuring, but I ran that thought through my head over and over the entire way home.

Old Khan's Palace

The call for Fajr prayer was sounding in the streets by the time I got home. It had taken me much longer to get back home than it had to get to Khan-ji's house. I was tired, in more ways than one. I was full and sleepy, but also felt like someone had wrung me out like a wet cloth after spending such a long time talking with Zoe. I didn't mind the feeling, but I had to keep stopping to sit a moment or two every few minutes on my way home. Finally, I reached my neighborhood, lazily waved at the daytime guard who let me in, slunk up our street, slipped in through our gate using my extra key, climbed the side of the house from the garden, and scrambled back into my room through my window. As I pulled my shoes off, I heard the water running in the bathroom. My door was still closed which meant that Ammi hadn't checked in on me yet. I quickly climbed into bed, closed my eyes, and fell asleep.

An hour later, (it felt like five minutes later), Ammi was shaking me awake and saying that I needed to pray and get ready for school. My head pounded and I felt dizzy as I walked into the bathroom and washed up. Splashing some cold water on my face woke me up a little bit, but then when I bowed my head to my mat while praying, I almost fell asleep again. I thought about asking Ammi if I could stay home from school that day so I could get some sleep, but I knew that she wouldn't let me unless I was sick. And anyway, there was a chance that Zoe might be back at school and I wanted to see him. After I got ready and had my breakfast, with a hot cup of chai to wake myself up a little more, Ammi drove me to school.

"Do you want me to pick you up today?" she asked when we pulled up in front of the school.

"No, I'll walk."

She looked at me with a bit of a sad look in her eyes.

"What's wrong?"

"I wish you'd let me pick you up one of these days."

I leaned over and kissed her on the cheek, "You can next week. I just feel like walking today, that's all."

And she smiled before giving me a quick peck on the forehead and shooing me out of the car, "Go, go, you'll be late!"

She waved at me before driving off and I stood there, waving at her car before it turned the corner and disappeared.

Once the car was gone, I turned towards the school gate and groaned as my head throbbed dull, before readjusting my bag over my shoulder and going inside.

I don't think a school morning had ever passed by as slowly for me before. I kept falling asleep in my classes, my Maths teacher finally hit me across the knuckles with a ruler to wake me up and then made me stand in the back of the classroom for the rest of class so that I'd stay awake. Even then, I could feel myself on the verge of falling asleep again. And in all of my classes, every time I looked at the clock, it looked like the time hadn't changed at all. It was all nothing but one long, slow and sleepy stretch until, finally, it was time for lunch. I usually ate my lunch in the cafeteria with everyone else, but I didn't feel like doing that this time. I was too tired to sit amongst all of the people and all of the noise, so I took my food and sat outside in one of the outdoor corridors, right at the edge of the school garden. Normally, I only went there to eat at the end of the year during exams time, I would sit and eat while studying. Sometimes Zoe would come with me and we would both quiz each other to get ready for our finals. Or rather, I quizzed him, and he goofed off and made up questions to ask me to entertain himself.

I sat there alone, eating my lunch and rocking back and forth slowly to keep myself awake while staring at the rosebushes. Just when I was starting to wonder why the school had planted specifically rose bushes, a shadow fell over my feet and an old woman's voice said, "Is anyone sitting with you, *sahib*?"

I grinned and looked up to see Zoe standing over me, I shook my head and he sat down next to me. Suddenly, I was wide awake.

"When'd you get here?" I asked.

"After first class ended, I woke up late," he admitted while fishing around in his pocket, "Khan-ji came and woke me up to tell me breakfast was ready and that's when I decided I'd drop by today." He finally found what he'd been looking for, a half squashed cigarette.

"What're you doing?!"

"What?" he asked innocently as he stuck it in between his lips and pulled his lighter out.

"We're at school!"

"I know where we are, I walked here all by myself," he lit the cigarette.

"You'll get caught!" I made a grab for the cigarette and he caught my wrist and stared at me with an amused expression on his face.

"What're you doing?"

"You'll get caught," I said again.

"Nobody's here, and if I see anyone coming, I'll put it out," he let go of my wrist, "You worry too much. How do you manage to sneak out of your house last night, walk through the city alone late at night to meet me, and still be this worried about something like a cigarette?"

"I'm talented," I said with a shrug and Zoe laughed.

While he smoked, I talked, "How're you feeling?"

"Fine."

"No, I mean, how're you feeling?"

"I said I feel fine," he looked at me and cocked an eyebrow, "Why do you keep asking me that?"

"I don't know, I guess I'm worried."

"Nothing to worry about," he said calmly.

I went quiet again and watched a beetle crawl along the edge of a leaf on one of the rosebushes while Zoe smoked silently.

"Class was different this morning."

I looked up at him, "What do you mean?"

He shrugged and flicked some ash off of his cigarette, "I don't know. Hard to explain. But it felt different. Usually everyone ignores me, I could be beaten to a pulp and they would just brush it off as me getting into something like I always do. But today...I don't know."

"Today they were watching you?" I asked.

"No, that's the thing. They weren't. But it felt like they were. I mean, they looked up when I walked in and Miss Sarah nodded at me and pointed to one of the seats in the back, that's all. But it felt like they were staring. Or talking. I don't know, it's hard to explain, but I could just feel something different."

He dropped his cigarette and put it out with his foot before picking it up and pocketing it.

"What'd you do that for?"

"I'll throw it away in a trash bin later, don't want to leave it lying around where a teacher might find it." He looked at me and I got a good look at his face, it didn't look that bad in the daylight. The cut going up through his eyebrow was still covered by the white strips of tape and the one along the bridge of his nose was covered as well, the swelling didn't even look as bad as it had in the dim light on the roof, but it was noticeable enough. And so was the bruising around his eye, which was the worst looking part of it all.

"I wish you could get away from her," I said.

Zoe looked surprised and he opened his mouth to respond, but before he could, a voice yelled out, "LOOK AT OUR SCHOOL'S FINEST MARRIED COUPLE!" followed by a bunch of loud laughter. Zoe and I both turned our heads to look up the walkway leading to where we were and saw Saad, one of Abdullah's friends, walking up the path along with a bunch of other boys. Most of the boys weren't friends with Abdullah, but they all hung around in one big group and referred to themselves as an entire gang, even though most of them weren't really friends. But they all sat together at lunch, smoked together in parks, drank together, and got into fights together. There were five of them coming our way including Saad. And as they approached I felt Zoe tense up next to me. They stopped and stood in the middle of the walking path, a few feet away from where we sat.

"What's the matter? Did we interrupt you?" asked Saad and the other boys laughed again. A tight knit pack of dogs.

"No, no. I've just got hearing trouble, why don't you come closer and say it again? Instead of standing all the way over there," Zoe said with a smile.

The smile on Saad's face fell and he looked wary, taunting Zoe was one thing, fighting him was another. But he recovered quickly and sneered, "What happened to your face? Did you and your husband fight or something?"

"Good one, but no. These aren't from a fight," Zoe gestured up at his face, "I can show you what a fight with me is like though, all you've got to do is come closer, like I said."

"I don't want to make you uglier than you already are."

"Ha!" Zoe pushed his hair back with his hand and nodded at Saad, "You could smash my face with a bat and I'd still look a whole lot better than you, ass."

There was a vein throbbing in Saad's temple, "You think you're so cool, don't you? You think everyone's impressed and afraid of you?" he hissed, "You think you can beat up everyone! Well, I see through you! You're full of shit!"

"And you're still talking," Zoe stood up and took a step forward, "Should I come over there and make it easier for the both of us?"

Saad stared at Zoe and took half a step back, all of the other boys were staring at Saad, waiting to see what he'd do next. There was a mixture of fear and hunger on their faces. They were afraid of what might happen next, but they still wanted to see it happen. Whatever *it* was.

I could feel the tension in the air, and I half stood up, ready to stop Zoe from doing anything stupid, but a few seconds passed by in silence, with nobody making a move. Finally, Saad shook his head and took another step back.

"Not here," he said, "Not where they can break it up as soon as it starts and then get me in trouble,"

"I don't see any teachers here," said Zoe with his arms extended out, as if he were inviting them all.

But Saad kept shaking his head and walking backwards, away from Zoe and I slowly, along with the rest of the boys. "Not here, not now, but soon. Somebody's going to get you soon, Zoe. You remember that. Everyone else will realize you're full of shit and somebody's going to do something about it." He turned around and started walking away with the rest of his group, and as they were leaving, Zoe leaned down, picked up a clod of dirt, and threw it at their backs. It exploded on top of Saad's head and he spun around, glaring at Zoe with hatred in his eyes. He looked like he was going to run back and pounce, but Zoe was standing there with his fists out in front of him, ready. Waiting. Saad spat on the ground and cursed Zoe before turning back around and walking away. Some of the other boys looked back at us as they were leaving, but they didn't say or do anything, then they turned the corner and they were gone.

Zoe stood there, staring at the spot where they'd been standing while I stared at his back, wondering what he'd do next. The sound of the bell to signal the end of lunch startled us both and as I gathered up my things, Zoe turned to look at me.

"Meet you out front at the end of the day?" he asked.

I nodded.

He grinned and clapped me on the shoulder before turning around and walking in the opposite direction, towards the upper class side of the building. I stood in that corridor for a moment, staring at the spot by the rosebush where Zoe had picked up that clod of dirt, and when the corridor started filling up with students headed to their next classes, I snapped out of it and melted into the crowd with the rest of them.

Zoe was standing by the school gate waiting for me when I walked out that afternoon. He had untucked his shirt, loosened his tie, and rolled his sleeves up. His school jacket was flung over one shoulder and he was leaning against the wall staring at all the cars speeding by on the road. As I approached, I thought he seemed kind of sad. But I must've imagined it, because when he saw me approaching, he flashed me a huge grin.

"Finally," he said, "I thought you'd be in there until nighttime."

"I was getting yelled at for sleeping in class," I told him.

Zoe laughed and clapped me on the back as we started walking, "Does that mean you're not up for any more late night rooftop tea parties?" he asked.

"Maybe not on school nights, I thought I was going to fall asleep standing up today."

He laughed and shook his head, "You get used to it after a while. Being in a sleepy state all the time, it's fun in a weird way."

"How is it fun?" I asked incredulously.

"Can't explain it, you have to be in it to know what I mean," he said with a shrug, "Anyway, do you want to go to Khan-ji's with me right now?" he asked.

"Right now? Won't he mind?"

Zoe shook his head.

"Um, well...I guess I could. I have to drop my stuff off at home, tell Ammi that I'm going to be with you, she'll have to meet you."

Zoe groaned loudly, "Why?"

"If I'm going to be with you, she has to meet you and know your face and stuff. You know how it is."

"Fine. But we won't have to stay for long will we?"

"She might make us eat something before we go. Actually, she probably will. Maybe some chai or something."

He groaned again, "Fine, fine, but you owe me. She won't uh, be upset about, you know..." I looked at him and he was pointing up at his bandages.

"No. She might ask you what happened. Just make something up. She'll probably talk to me about it later."

Zoe let out a sigh, "If I had known I'd be meeting your mother today, I'd've worn my best suit."

I threw a punch to my side, hitting his shoulder and he laughed.

As we talked, we cut away from the roads and started walking along sides of neighborhoods and apartment buildings, pretty soon, we turned into an alleyway to take a shortcut to my house.

"I wanted to ask you," I said, "That thing that you were talking about last night. About riding your bike out at night...I was wondering, could I come with you some time?"

"Want to experience it for yourself, huh?" he smirked.

I nodded.

"Of course you can come with me," he said with a smile, "We'll do it sometime soon. I promise."

We were so wrapped up in our conversation that we almost didn't hear the whistle, but Zoe fell silent and stopped walking. I stopped too and the both of us heard it again, a low whistle followed by the sound of laughter. And before he jumped down from the wall, I knew who it was. Abdullah landed in front of us and brushed some of the dirt off of his hands. Zoe and I both looked up to our left and saw five or six other boys also sitting up on the wall, they jumped down and landed in front of us too. I took a step back and felt myself be shoved forward, I turned around and saw Saad and another boy standing behind us.

Saad had a look of satisfaction on his face, he stared at Zoe grinning big, like a wild dog that had just found the next meal.

"I told you someone was gonna get you soon," hissed Saad.

Zoe looked back at him cooly without saying anything and then turned back to face Abdullah and the rest standing in front of us.

"Are you trying to scare us, Abdullah?" Zoe asked calmly.

Abdullah took a cigarette out of his mouth and stepped on it, grinding it into the dirt, "Scare you? No. I've decided that you need to learn why you shouldn't mess with us."

"Yeah? And who's going to teach me? All eight of you together?" Zoe reached into his pocket as he spoke, pulled out his lighter, and started flicking it, "I probably won't get you all, but I'm not going down until one of you idiots is blinded."

Abdullah and the other boys eyed the lighter, just as they had the other day, but this time Abdullah smiled, "That big talk isn't going to help you today, not against me," he took a step forward and rolled his sleeves up too.

A look of surprised flickered across Zoe's face for a moment but then that smirk of his crept onto his face and put the lighter back in his pocket. "Oh," he said before taking a step forward himself.

I wanted to reach out and stop him, but my arms wouldn't move, I took in a sharp breath and took a step backwards. This time, I didn't bump into Saad. He and the other boy had moved back too, and so had all of the boys that had been standing in front of us. There was a sort of walled in circle now, the high alley wall to the left, the back of one of the apartment buildings on the right, and the only way out of the alley was either forward or backwards, and Saad, the other boy, and I stood blocking the way backwards, and six more boys stood blocking the way forward. Zoe and Abdullah stood in the middle, only a few feet apart, circling each other slowly. I wanted to leave, I didn't want to see this, but I knew Saad and all of the other boys wouldn't let me go, they wanted me to watch. They *all* wanted to watch, the wild anticipation on their faces radiated into the air and created a bubble of energy in that alleyway. Only I didn't feel excited, I felt sick and scared, my arms and legs felt like lead, as if I were the one fighting. But I wasn't, Zoe was. And so was Abdullah. And if either of them felt the same way I did, they didn't show it.

"I've wanted to do this for years," hissed Abdullah as he and Zoe circled each other.

"What was stopping you?" said Zoe with a bit of amusement in his voice.

Abdullah clenched his jaw and his face twisted into a mask of anger. Hatred.

"Fight already!" shouted one boy.

And then they did.

Abdullah swung first, lunging forward with a yell and swinging his right fist at Zoe's face. Zoe stepped back before the punch connected and Abdullah's fist barely grazed Zoe's chin. Abdullah stumbled forward as he missed and Zoe brought up his left fist up in a diagonal punch, Abdullah turned his head at the last second and the punch caught him on the ear. There was a loud smack and a yell of pain from Abdullah, who went to his knees and grabbed Zoe around the legs. They both went down, but Zoe landed on his rear and wrapped his one arm around Abdullah's neck and then brought the elbow of his other arm down at the base of Abdullah's neck repeatedly.

There were more, smothered yells of pain from Abdullah and he desperately clawed up at Zoe's face, trying to dig his nails into his eyes and mouth to escape. They both scooted on the ground and wound up pressed against the back wall of the building. Abdullah's hands got a grip on Zoe's hair and slammed his head back into the wall. Zoe cried out loudly and let go of Abdullah, reaching up to clutch his own head. Abdullah rolled away in the dirt and quickly scrambled to his feet, rubbing his neck and bleeding from the ear.

"Hit him!" shouted the boys, "Hit him again! Come on Abdullah!"

Zoe got back up to his feet as Abdullah charged forward again and this time, Zoe stepped to the side and grabbed him coming in by the shirt collar with both hands and flung him towards the back wall where his head had just been. Abdullah's body crunched against the wall and he fell in a heap on the ground, everyone groaned loudly and Zoe took a few steps back.

"That's it. Let's end it," he said.

Abdullah pushed himself back up to his feet and shook his head, "Fuck you!" he yelled before charging forward *again*. Zoe crouched and braced himself, this time Abdullah tackled him and slammed him hard up against the alley wall. Zoe kept himself standing and Abdullah kept his arms wrapped around Zoe's body, keeping them both standing up. They both grappled with each other like that for a few seconds until Abdullah freed one of his arms and swung up at Zoe's face. This time, he caught him right under the black eye, and then he slammed an open hand right into bridge of Zoe's bandaged nose. Zoe cried out loudly and let go of Abdullah, who took a step back and grinned menacingly at Zoe, who was doubled over and clutching his face.

"Do you give up?" asked Abdullah as his friends cheered.

I felt sick to my stomach and glanced over at Saad staring at
Zoe against the wall with a huge grin on his face.

"I asked you a question, ass!"

Zoe stayed doubled over and Abdullah stepped forward and
grabbed him by the hair which turned out to be a big mistake.
Zoe immediately straightened up and grabbed Abdullah by the
back of the neck and pulled him in while driving his own head
forward. There was a dull thud and a sickening crack, like
someone throwing an egg against the wall, followed by a howl of
pain from Abdullah who stumbled and fell backwards. He was
holding his nose with both hands and blood was flowing freely
through his fingers. All of the boys had fallen silent. Zoe glared
down at him as Abdullah pushed himself backwards, he glared up
at Zoe from the ground and took his hands away from his face.
There was a deep cut going along the bridge of the nose and
Abdullah's nose itself had been knocked to an odd angel. Broken.
Completely broken along the bridge.

"You're crazy," said Abdullah in a thick voice.

"We're done here," said Zoe coldly.

I opened my mouth to say something but I was knocked to
the side as Saad rushed past me at Zoe. I grabbed at his arm to
hold him back, but he swung me around and threw me to the
ground. He swung wildly at Zoe's face, but Zoe caught both of
his arms coming in and pulled him in close, holding him in place
for a split second before driving his knee up hard into Saad's

stomach. Saad went limp and fell over onto his side, curling up and wheezing loudly, trying to get some air back into his lungs.

All of the other boys watched silently as Zoe stared down at Saad with a look of disgust on his face, I stood and watched silently from where I'd landed when Saad had thrown me down. I brushed the dirt off of my pants and waited for something else to happen. For someone to say something. But nobody did. That feeling that had been in the air was gone now, and my arms and legs felt jelly-like. I wasn't sure if I'd be able to take a single step without falling over. But right as I was getting ready to call out to Zoe and get him to leave now, there was a small clicking noise. I looked to my right and saw Abdullah standing a couple feet away from me, with one hand clutching his nose again, and the other hand pointing a small revolver at Zoe.

"What're you doing?!" shouted some of the other boys, "Put that away Abdullah!"

"Shut up!" he snapped at him without taking his eyes off of Zoe.

My eyes darted back and forth from Zoe to Abdullah, Zoe was staring at the pistol with a look on his face that I had never seen before. Fear. And his fear seemed to spread in that little alleyway and create a new bubble so that everyone felt it. Even Abdullah looked afraid, his hand was shaking and when he spoke, I could hear a hint of fear that he was trying to mask with anger. He was uncertain of what to do next.

"Abdullah..." I said quietly.

"SHUT UP!" he roared.

Zoe took a slow step backwards and spoke calmly, "It's just a fight," he said.

"You broke my fucking nose!" yelled Abdullah.

"So you're going to shoot me?"

No response.

"Are you?" Zoe asked again.

I could feel my body being charged with energy, nervous energy. I had to move. Do something. Something was about to happen, I could feel it in my bones. I had to move. Zoe had to move. Abdullah had to move. Somebody had to move!

"Abdullah?" Saad spoke softly from the ground, staring up at Abdullah.

Just for a second, Abdullah took his eyes off of Zoe and glanced down at Saad, and in that second, I finally reacted. I bolted to where Zoe was standing, faster than I'd ever moved before I think, and there were yells, curses maybe, but I didn't hear them right. It was as if though somebody had muffled all of the sound in the world and I saw Abdullah turn to look at me in slow motion, with surprise in his eyes. And I felt my arm move towards his face. And I felt my fist collide with his jaw. And I could feel myself jump on him as he fell. But as we both went down, the silence broke. An explosion cut through it. And then the sound came back. Yells. Cursing. A scream of pain.
The bubble of fear popped. Panic took over. And my arm was moving on its own. Hitting Abdullah in the face over and over,

pinning his gun arm down with my other hand. There was a ringing in my ears. I could hear the blood pounding, my heart beating, Abdullah screaming in pain. And then someone pulled me off.

They were saying something, I couldn't understand.

"Look!" he yelled.

It was one of the boys who had been blocking our path.

"Look!" and he pointed this time, and I looked.

Saad was holding someone, yelling up at the other boys who surrounded them.

"Go get help!" he was yelling, "Tell someone!"

I ran forward and pushed the other boys out of the way, pushed Saad out of the way too.

Zoe was on the ground and his face was twisted with pain. It hadn't been an explosion that I'd heard, it was the sound of the gun going off. And the bullet had hit Zoe in the leg. He was holding his knee with both hands but the blood was seeping through, staining his pants, the dirt around him, everything. He looked pale. Sick. And he was sweating.

"Ali is getting help," said Saad nervously.

I ignored him.

"Zoe?" I held his head in my arms and pressed one hand down on top of his two to try and slow the bleeding, "Zoe?" I said again.

"How bad is it?" he kept his eyes on me.

I shook my head, "Just a scratch," I said without looking at his leg, "They're getting help. You'll be okay, don't worry. It's just a scratch."

His bottom lip trembled and he let out a hiss of pain.

"Feels worse," he mumbled, "Feels a lot worse."

Three months later, I stood at the bus station with Zoe, who sat in his wheelchair with his right leg propped out straight in front of him and covered in a white cast.

"You get it taken off in a month right?" I asked.

He nodded.

"Do you think you'll have gotten used to Quetta by then?"

"I don't know."

"You'll start rehabbing there too?"

He nodded.

"And then you go to Australia with Aisha, right?"

He nodded again and said, "Won't be able to walk on my own again though. Doctor said I'll have to use a cane."

"Well...maybe that'll only be for a little while?" I said.

"Yeah. Maybe."

The two of us fell silent again and I glanced up at the big clock hanging above the waiting benches where a bunch of people were sitting. Five minutes till the bus was supposed to arrive.

"I'm going to miss you," he said suddenly.

I looked back down at Zoe, "I'm going to miss you too."

"I probably won't be coming back, you know that right?" he asked, looking up at me.

I nodded and crouched down in front of him so I could look him directly in the eye, "But I know I'll see you again," I said.

"How?"

"I just do. It's a feeling."

Zoe sighed and looked to the side, I could see a vein throbbing in his temple. He did that a lot now. He would go quiet and the vein in his temple would throb. As if his thoughts were getting ready to burst out of his skull and spill out into the open. His hair was shorter now. There were no thick, dark curls falling to his shoulders anymore. He'd gotten it buzzed down nearly all the way, his head was covered in coarse, dark stubble now. And he had lost weight, he didn't look like he used to. He looked shrunken now, liked he'd been sucked dry. Drained. And he always looked pale now, weak, like he was on the verge of passing out all the time.

"Bus still not here?" a girl's voice cut through my thoughts and we both turned to look at her.

Zoe's older sister, Aisha, stood there clutching her bag in one hand and a sandwich in the other. She handed the sandwich to Zoe, "They only had chicken," she said apologetically.

"That's fine," he said as he took the sandwich from her, "I'll eat it on the bus."

"It's still not here yet?" she asked again.

"Almost," I said.

As I said it, the bus pulled up in front of us, hissing to a slow stop and opening one of the side doors near the back. A man in a white uniform holding a clipboard jumped out and walked over to where we were standing, "Rana family?" he asked, looking down at his clipboard.

Aisha nodded.

The man smiled, "I'm your attendant, follow me," he turned and went behind the bus, he reached up and opened the back door, pulled down a ramp, and waved us over.

"You'll go in through here, your seats are in the back," he said to Aisha.

"Thank you," said Aisha and the man bowed his head and stepped to the side, waiting for them to get on.

Aisha began to push Zoe's chair up the ramp but he held his hand up to stop her, "Hold on a second," he said.

She stepped back and Zoe turned to look at me, I leaned down and he grabbed me, pulling me down into a hug. And I wrapped my arms around him as best I could, hugging him back.

"You sure about that feeling of yours?" he asked.

"Dead certain," I said, smiling into his shoulder.

He kissed the top of my head and let me go, and when I stepped back I saw that he was crying.

"You'll be okay Zoe," I said, "And we *will* see each other again. It's not like I have any other friends to replace you with."

He laughed at that and then, he took his ring off of his finger and threw it up at me, "Catch."

I caught it with both hands and stared at him, "What's this for?"

"Just in case," he said with a smile.

"Zoe I can't take this, it's your ring!"

"Keep it. I'm not letting you give it back, just because I'm in this chair doesn't mean I can't still take you on you know," he flashed me with one of his smirks, the first I'd seen since before the fight with Abdullah, and I almost burst into tears on the spot.

I nodded and put the ring on my right ring finger, "How's it look?" I asked while holding my hand up.

"Perfect."

I smiled at him and he smiled back for the last time before turning and nodding at Aisha, who had been watching us with a strange little smile on her face. She grabbed the chair and started pushing it up the ramp, she paused at the top and turned to look at me, "Take care of yourself Amir."

"Take care of him," I said

She nodded and stepped through the back door, the attendant closed and locked it behind them.

I stepped back, watching as everyone else slowly filed onto the bus. Once everyone was on, the doors closed and I searched the back windows for their faces. I decided that they must've been sitting in the far back past the windows once I couldn't find Aisha's or Zoe's face. I shoved my hands into my pockets, playing with the ring using my thumb, and watched as the bus slowly pulled away from the station. Even though I couldn't see them as it began to drive away, I used one arm to wave at the bus. I don't know why. It made me feel a bit better though. And when they were finally so far up the main road that I couldn't see them from where I was standing anymore, I put my arm down and started walking back home.

It was a weekend, so I could take as long as I liked getting home. Ammi and Abba were both home, waiting for me. They'd both said their goodbyes to Zoe that morning, when the taxi came to get us all and bring us to the bus station. Abba told me that he took the day off because he was feeling sick lately, but after he'd gone to bed the night before, Ammi had told me that he wanted to see Zoe off and he was worried about me. But he would never tell me that himself, for some reason. Zoe had said his goodbyes to his parents before coming to our house that morning, I didn't ask him how it went, and he didn't tell me much. Just that his mother had cried. But then, she'd been crying often since he'd gotten shot, so that wasn't new.

So much had changed since that day. Abdullah was in jail. Abba had been the arresting officer. He'd told me that Abdullah cried about how sorry he was when they'd taken him in, but I couldn't tell if he was making it up or not. He'd seemed fine to me at the trial, I'd been a witness. Along with Saad and all of the other boys. It all seemed so warped and twisted, as if it wasn't a real thing at all. I might be waking up in a while, realizing it'd all been some long and strange dream and that Zoe's okay and not in a wheelchair and Abdullah is still just some bully.

I pulled my hand out of my pocket and looked at Zoe's ring. My ring now. I stroked the black stone lightly with my thumb and suddenly felt hot tears falling down my face. I was crying and I couldn't tell why. It wasn't one thing. It was everything. And maybe the ring was the only reason I'd have to think about Zoe ever again. I swallowed hard and reached up to wipe my tears away. I decided I couldn't go home yet, not like this. But there was one place I could go, maybe the only place I could go. The only person who could maybe understand how I felt, because maybe his goodbye to Zoe hadn't been enough for him either...

Half an hour later, I stood in front of Khan-ji's house, staring at the front door. Slowly, I reached up with my right hand and knocked on the door. A few seconds went by before the door swung open, and Khan-ji stood there, looking exactly the way he had that night three months before when I'd come to have chai with Zoe. Except his clothes were a dark brown now, not light blue. He was still hunched over. Still had that walking stick in one hand.

He stared at me silently and I stared back for a moment before clearing my throat and saying in Pashto, "He's gone."

Khan-ji's lips stretched into a sad little smile, "He started teaching you Pashto?" he asked.

I nodded.

He let out a heavy sigh and nodded before reaching up and taking off his *pakol*, he ran a hand back through his hair before placing the *pakol* back on his head. Then he put the hand on my shoulder and stepped aside, "Come in," he said.

I stepped inside and Khan-ji closed the door behind me.

"Would you like some chai?" he asked.

I nodded.

"Sit at the table, I was just about to make some."

I went over and sat down at the little dining table in the corner. While Khan-ji put the water on the stove to boil, I started played with the ring again. I almost didn't notice when he pulled a chair out and sat down across from me.

"Are you okay?" he asked.

"I'm not sure."

"Let it out."

"I don't know where to begin," I mumbled.

He reached over and placed one of those large, scarred hands on top of mine and I looked up at him, he had that sad little smile on his face again.

"Anywhere is fine," he looked up at the clock on the wall, "We've got plenty of time."

Made in the USA
Middletown, DE
06 November 2016